Introduction

I was born in Portsmouth in 1961. Dad worked in the Dockyard and the family lived across the harbour in Gosport, or to be more precise, behind the Gasworks wall.

Over forty years on and I couldn't be further from my previous life, living in a remote Welsh valley with my husband Mick, trying to get back to a more simple life, working to live rather than living to work.

This book is hopefully an amusing and interesting account of how the escape to the country came about and follows the first few years spent working to create a smallholding and become as self sufficient as possible by adapting to life in a remote rural setting, far away from the street lights and urban life we left behind.

It tells of learning to keep pigs and chickens, lambing, a never to be repeated attempt to artificially inseminate a very big and very indignant sow, almost flattening the cottage with an enormous felled oak tree and the joy of seeing our first born piglets happily suckling. Littered throughout with recipes for hedgerow wines and preserves for light relief!

Whether you read every page or skip to the alcohol I hope you enjoy the experience and don't get a headache!

Hope all is well in your world

Jane Crane

Jane Crane

From
City Strife
to
Rural Life

Jane Crane: From City Strife to Rural Life

First published in Great Britain in 2011
By Jane Crane

Jane Crane has asserted her right
to be identified as the author of this work

Cover design and all photographs
by Jane and Mick Crane

ISBN 978-1-4477-2223-6

This book is dedicated to:

Dad, who would have loved life in the valley

To

Mum for her love and support in everything we do

And to

Mick, my husband and best pal, the journey would be meaningless without him. I love him to bits, even if he will be mortified to see it put in print!

One day at a time Sweet Jesus
That's all I'm asking of you
Give me the strength to do everything
That I have to do.
Yesterday's gone Sweet Jesus
And tomorrow may never be mine
Help me today and show me the way
One day at a time

@ Marijohn Wilkins/Kris Kristofferson

Contents

Mid life crisis	1
Back to basics	4
Chasing the dream	7
This is it	11
Lorries, loading and we're off!	18
Escape to the new country	22
Reality bites	27
Home on the range & unwanted guests	30
Boys Toys (essential kit for the smallholder!)	33
Planning the plot	36
A taste of the country	38
Tree taming	41
A load of bullocks	44
Animal outbuildings	49
Big Pig	51
Chicken picking	57
Pride goes before a fall	61
Piggy pregnancy, piglets, piglets and yet more piglets!	63
Trees and telephone lines don't mix	71
From old pond to piggy heaven	74
Sheep at last!	78
The circle of life	84
From pigs to princes	88
Lambing live!	91
Frisky, fleeced and beaten by the weather	96
Juggling sheep	103

Tupping time and pleasuring pigs!	107
Lambs come of age	111
The big freeze	114
Happy Christmas, eventually!	118
Our first New Year as smallholders	121
Keeping warm and snow, snow and more snow	125
Porkers depart and sheep surprise	132
Natures way	135
Mad March	141
Pig poo and newborns	145
Freedom and frights for the chucks	147
Fluffy White and the Birthday Girls lamb at last	150
Weaners to porkers	153
Hardstandings and hounds	159
Dagging the lambs	162
Unexpected early Christmas presents	164
The lull before the storm	172
Happy New Year – back to reality	178

Mid life crisis

Great quote from John Lennon sums it up 'Life is what happens when you are busy making plans'. It took until well past our forties to realise this, perhaps it takes that long to really appreciate how much life means to you, having less time in front than behind is an alarming wake up call. I guess that's the reason for the mid life crisis, the feeling life is passing you by and making you want to feel you are really living life and not just going through the motions.

Life seemed so simple as teenagers in the 70s, everything mapped out for us. Leave school, get a job, find your own place, have a family, live happy ever after. Bang on cue, Mick and I fell for each other in our final years at school, leaving at sixteen to work in Portsmouth for the MOD and District Valuers office, working hard to save a deposit for our first house. Without knowing it we had joined the rat race and happily started running the treadmill towards the 'happy ever after.' We spent the next thirty years on the same route, although children were not to be, work and everyday living took over. Townies, born and bred, our moves around the South of England from Hampshire to Surrey to Oxfordshire were all work related and based in or close to the city or town we were working in. For the last seven years we had lived in Charlton on Otmoor, a village nestled in commuter heaven between the M40 and A34. Great rural scenery with all urban benefits close to hand, Bicester Factory Outlet shopping centre and town shops in one direction and Oxford City retail therapy within equal distance in the other.

My office had recently moved to a new business park just off the Oxford ring road, rapidly filling with government agencies relocating from the city centre. The 7 mile commute could now take up to two hours due to the traffic congestion, made much worse by the bright spark who planned the business park, designing only one road in and out. To avoid gridlock meant really early starts and late finishes. I was now in charge of the office, deskbound with office targets and personnel issues my main role. The technical stuff was fine; it was the growth industry of return statistics and non-productive management systems together with endless personnel problems that were sapping my spirit. It was getting harder to take serious the things people seemed to relish in making problems out of, one morning I was met with an indignant delegation wanting me to sort out a colleague's personal hygiene problem, 'she smells, what are you going to do about it?' give me a break, life's too short!!

My flippancy and irritation was mainly due to current circumstances, which were causing us to doubt whether what we were doing was how we really wanted to live for the rest of our lives. Mick had recently gone self employed and was having to work all hours to get established and my best friend in the village, Beat, had recently passed away and I was having great trouble adjusting to life without her. Living a long way from family, Beat had been like a second mum. Her cottage was opposite ours in the lane and we had a cup of tea every morning and called out good night to each other last thing at night. I felt unsettled without her but at a loss to know how to resolve it. Then our beloved old German Shepherd, Kip, died; she was with us from eight weeks old to ten years. We missed her so much, the house seemed empty without her; she always lifted our spirits when we were feeling down, without her our walks were not the same. In comparison the petty trials and tribulations at work really didn't seem a priority, our life lacked focus, we had lost our way.

Happily, life doesn't stand still and we were quickly jolted out of our rut by the unexpected arrival of a lunatic German Shepherd called Tia who turned our lives upside down. She chased Mick down the lane and he was smitten, he found out she was the unwanted dog of the pub landlord who was relocating the next day and by the end of the afternoon he brought her home. A rescue dog, she had been kept chained up as a pup and whilst at the pub shut in a pen outside during the day, regularly escaping and desperately following walkers in search of company, not knowing how to play, trust or receive affection. We had our work cut out with her as she was 4 yrs old, never been on a lead and had never known the company of other dogs so went ballistic whenever she saw them. Every house in the village seemed to have one or two dogs that were walked off the lead around the same routes and as soon as Tia caught sight of them she was off, barking incessantly until they disappeared from sight, towing us along behind her.

We totally outside our comfort zone, had to rearrange everything to work with Tia, focusing on helping her overcome her fear of contact and commitment. At least as Mick was self employed he was able to have her with him almost 24/7, they developed a mutually supportive friendship, he was so patient with her and she gradually opened up and gave him her trust and affection, becoming his shadow, wherever he went she was at his side, only the bathroom door affording him any privacy! At night she curled up on an old armchair overlooking our bed, contentedly watching over us. Tia now seemed totally settled, living each day to the full and it was the kick we needed to find a way to change our lives and do likewise.

Back to basics

Our first step was to take some time to think, away from the day-to-day routine and all social trappings. Mick had finally completed his long-term project, a 1969 classic VW Bay Camper he rebuilt from total wreckage. This was to be our escape vehicle and holiday home for three weeks back to basics, touring the North Cornish coast. The size of the van would definitely test our commitment to travelling light and living simply, especially as Tia seemed to have more kit than we did!

We had a wonderful time walking the coastal path from Padstow to Woolacombe. The more remote we were the better we liked it. Sitting around a campfire at the end of each stress free day the conversation often turned to how idyllic it would be if life could always be so simple, no streetlights, no shops, no traffic noise or crowds, just concentrating on having what you needed, rather than all the things you were convinced you had to have.

A lot to be said for the simple life, though striking the balance between what we had and what we really wanted, kept us chatting as the sun set, a new moon rose and the stars came out.

We started comparing what we had at home with what we needed to get by, from the number of rooms in the house to clothes in the wardrobes, the latter a brilliant example of materiality overtaking reality! Then we talked about what made us happiest and were pleasantly reassured that we valued the same things, quality time together, living simply without the pressure to conform to others' opinions of how you should live, getting pleasure from making things rather than buying them. By the final evening just as the sun set in a blaze of orange and red flames our 'epiphany' was complete, we wanted to opt out of the rat race, downsize, get back to basics and live as self sufficiently as possible.

On our return home we started Googling 'Smallholding' sites, it became clear quite quickly that even our simple ideal, a small cottage with at least an acre in Cornwall or Devon was far beyond our financial means, as was anything in the South or middle England. Still in escape mode we planned another touring holiday to mid Wales, as one of my work team argued that the Pembroke coast was much better than Cornwall and that the unspoiled beauty of mid and west Wales was well worth a visit. Checking websites for Welsh properties with an acre or more of land we were pleasantly surprised to see that prices were almost half those we had been looking at in England, falling significantly in the more remote western rural areas. I was excited at the thought our dream could become a reality, albeit in a different country, though the voice of reason, Mick, suggested this visit would be purely to explore, as it was one thing to move locally, another to up sticks to another country far away from any safety net.

Only one road was needed to take us all the way from Oxford to the Pembroke coast, the A40, mainly dual carriageway, the biggest hold up was trying to get past the Oxford ring road. It was a beautiful journey through the best of the English and Welsh countryside, via Cheltenham to Gloucester, through the Forest of Dean to Ross on Wye, Monmouth, Brecon, Llandovery, Carmarthen and onto the coast at St Clear where we stopped off to climb up to Dylan Thomas's boathouse where it was claimed he wrote 'Under Milkwood', and to camp in a farmer's field in walking distance of the famous Pendine sands, eight miles of sandy beach, which in its heyday was used for speed trials.

My workmate was right; the coastline views both out to sea and inland were spectacular. We travelled further West staying in small field sites along the way, all the way round to St David's and Abarearon, spending days on golden sands, exploring cliffs and sampling wonderful brews and lunches at hostelries off the beaten track. The roads, in many places rough tracks, were uncluttered and the towns and villages lacked the urban frenzy of their English counterparts. All the locals were really friendly, changing from Welsh to English language as soon as they heard us speak, happy to tell us about the area and give us directions to the best places to see or stay. I loved the gentle singsong accents, even if they were talking about us in Welsh we wouldn't mind because it sounded so nice!

Something else that was great was the unrestricted access to so much heritage. In England whether within stately homes or at a monument on a rocky crag there will be roped off areas for you to stand behind and pay for the privilege to view from a distance, not so in West Wales. From being invited to try out the servant quarter's beds in Dinefwr House to wandering through the Cathedral grounds at St David's and forgotten lead mines along the way the experience was totally hands on. The complete lack of containment and bureaucracy was refreshing and made each experience more real, we felt the history and sense of place and were starting to hope we could become part of it.

Chasing the dream

Our evenings round the camp fire were spent discussing whether we were on the verge of a life changing decision or whether we should stick with our original plan to put off any change for five years, at which time we would finish our mortgage and hit 50. As Mick had recently gone self-employed he thought that if we were to make a change it should be now before he became established and tied to relying on others for an income again. I happily agreed, I was feeling increasingly frustrated, my job now totally deskbound, whereas before I was always out on site or negotiating valuations with agents, responsible for my own workload but without responsibility for others. Spurred by thoughts of mortality and swayed by the fact that my department had offices in Wales, which may enable a transfer, we started to think that our dream might be able to become a reality. If, and it was a big if, by downsizing and going West we could pay off the mortgage then the saving on payments would offset one wage and enable us to build up a small holding. The other wage, by living simply and being as self sufficient as possible, would hopefully be enough to pay the bills. Feeling quite light headed, and this time not from the cider, we decided it was now or never and spent the next day travelling between Carmarthen and Abergavenny to visit the local estate agents to see if we were chasing a pipe dream. The two towns, located along the A40 covered the area we had decided would be within reach of my offices in Merthyr, Carmarthen and at a push Swansea.

One day, 15 agents and 60 miles later we were sat outside the van on a camp site in Llandovery on the edge of the Brecon Beacons National Park, working our way through an enormous pile of maps and particulars. Other than price our only criteria had been something out of towns with more than an acre of land, perhaps we should have mentioned with a habitable property, which could be reached by something other than a helicopter. We discounted the large number of derelict stone buildings presented as 'development opportunities'. Next we weeded out anything described as 'secluded', the maps showed that this was agent speak for a very remote location, normally in the middle of forestry land with access more suited to mountain goats than cars.

After these exclusions, together with those totally above our price range, which agents feel compelled to throw in just to make you feel totally inadequate, we ended up with five, all in Carmarthenshire, which at face value we thought looked promising. The properties ranged from a farmhouse with 35 acres to a house with a shower block and camping field, all suspiciously within our budget. We decided that as we had a week of holiday left we would spend the next two days viewing the properties, just to see if they lived up to the hype of the agent's particulars.

First on the list, unsurprisingly, was the 35-acre farmhouse near St Clear. Disappointingly we found the 35 acres were in the middle of a family dispute, and subject to ongoing legal wrangling, may or may not be available. As the property was landlocked by the family who farmed and lived in the houses surrounding it we decided living in the middle of a clan war would not be ideal and so we crossed it off our list. Next was a house within the Brecon Beacons National Park, which had a campsite field. We got lost trying to find this; several times missing the turning and musing on how any prospective campers might find the elusive site. At least an hour or so from the A40, in the middle of nowhere, some two hours from Swansea or Carmarthen it would be a pain for commuting. Still, Mick was already making plans for converting the barn to a garage and expanding the shower block so we contacted the agent to find out more only to be told that the vendor was in no hurry to sell and was very hard to get hold of, begging the question of why bother putting it on the market? One more for the bin.

The next three properties took us so far north of Carmarthen and stretched the description 'rural idyll' to the limit; even the guys in the film 'Deliverance' wouldn't have ventured to some of them. We returned to our favourite campsite at Llandovery to chill out for a while. The small market town at the crossroads of the old drovers' trails from West and North Wales to the South was still a farming centre with weekly livestock markets, giving a real sense of community. Walking through we found the estate agent in the main street was not one we had come across and we found two houses within our range, the first a farmhouse with some 5 acres in the Towy valley, north of Llandovery. The agent gave us details to get there, saying although secluded it was easy to find, alarm bells should have rung but we liked the idea of driving the old drovers trails up the valley to finish off the day and the second place, a little white cottage, which looked like a chapel offering a paddock and 'rough land' in a hamlet called Rhandirmwyn, was on the way back so we decided it would be worth taking with us.

The Rhandirmwyn road followed the old drovers' trail leading up to Lynn (Lake) Brianne, a 300 acre reservoir at the head of the Towy valley and on through the aptly named Devils staircase pass to Tregaron and beyond to the west coast or east to Builth Wells. The road was surfaced but had no pavements and was very windy, with many passing spaces where it became too narrow to safely pass. We gently climbed the seven miles to Rhandirmwyn, each corner revealing an equally beautiful view to the one just left. Rising hills chequered with a patchwork of fields and woodland of more shades of green than we had ever seen, occupied alternately by sheep, cattle and scattered farmhouses. Red kites flew high overhead, squirrels dashed madly across the road whilst the odd sheep ambled alongside convinced the grass was greener outside their fence. It was surreal, occasionally we passed a tractor, camper van or forestry lorry loaded with timber, reminding us this was the 20th century, otherwise we fully expected a coach and horses to round the bend followed by drovers' flocks of geese on the way to market!

The drop on my side of the road was quite dramatic, rock cut away to the water flowing below to join the river Towy from which the valley got its name. We finally reached a sign for Rhandirmwyn village and came to four houses with a small post office/shop next to the Royal Oak pub. Our directions were to keep going until we reached a sign for the Towy Bridge Inn at which we were to turn left over the Towy Bridge and then continue on the road until we arrived at the farmhouse. By the time we got to the bridge we knew this was a step too far for any daily commute, but having come this far thought we would at least see the house. Going over the metal bridge we were quite disappointed not to see a banjo duel, it definitely felt as though we were entering no mans land. A feeling not dispelled as we carried on climbing up an even narrower road thickly lined with trees, winding from bend to bend without any passing spaces. After twenty minutes of rallying from corner to corner to avoid meeting anything we spotted the estate agents board laying at the roadside adjacent to a very muddied farm gate entrance giving access to a very steep rocky track up a vertical slope into more woodland. We looked at each other and in mutual agreement decided whatever was up there it was definitely not for us unless it had a helicopter and landing strip thrown in. Yes we wanted to be off the beaten track but not beaten by it!

Time was getting on so rather than going back to Llandovery we followed signs for a camp site, back past the Towy Bridge Inn, out of the woodland and into the open beauty of the valley spreading out below us. Turning left we had a wonderful view of the Rhandirmwyn side of the valley, with the river Towy flowing through the bottom, a campsite alongside the far side of the riverbank, with a church beyond and a smattering of scattered houses along the lane leading back to the post office and pub we had first passed. It looked an idyllic place for rest and inspiration so we headed downwards, crossing the shallow bridge and into the campsite for the night.

It was a camping and caravan club site so only a small office and shower block evidenced any commercial use. We picked a spot next to the river; the sound of the water flowing past was really relaxing, as was watching the flock of sheep grazing on the opposite bank. We quickly set up camp and sat outside to make the most of the setting sun and relax, not difficult with the amazing views up the valley either side of the Towy. In direct contrast to the shades of green was what looked like an undulating grey rock formation alongside the boundary opposite the river. The camp warden told us it was actually spoil heaps, a reminder of a bygone lead mining age for which the valley was famous. The site, known locally as 'The Crusher' used to house the buildings and machinery for crushing the lead. Ore was brought down from the Rhandirmwyn lead mine further up the valley by horse and dram. The lead was taken out of the crushed ore and the heaps were the spoil left over. The mine closed in 1936 and the site had remained unused since. We learned the site was out of bounds to the campsite as it was privately owned, belonging to a cottage, which was for sale, called 'Pen y Gorof' on the dram way, the same lane as the church, St Barnabas, above. Our ears picked up, this was the little white house we had the details for, at least now we knew what the agent's 'rough land' referred to and the warden's tales convinced us this was one place we definitely wanted to check out.

This is it!!

The next morning armed with the sales particulars we walked Tia up to the Church, St Barnabas at the top of the lane leading to Pen y Gorof.

The lane was single track and pot holed with a dead end sign rather deterring taking a car down. As we walked down squirrels criss crossed the path, driving Tia crazy, not knowing which direction to run first. The lane was lined with a mixture of old oak, maple and blackthorn in varying autumn colours, to the right side the land fell away to the Crusher site and to the left revealed a very large overgrown area which in a past life had been a holding pond, providing water via a sluice under the lane to drive the water wheel which ran the crusher machinery with the added benefit of providing a washing area for the mineworkers.

Rounding a corner we got our first view of the cottage. It looked very tiny but full of character, set behind a store.

We couldn't resist having a look at the front of the cottage, especially as the little white picket fence gate was hanging invitingly open.

Following an old sunken brick pathway winding past the front porch and into the front garden we were bowled over by the little cottage's character, complete with roses growing all around the front porch it looked a picture. The front garden, alongside the lane, sloped down to two timber outbuildings and a little gate back onto the lane.

At the side of the garden was a higher level overgrown area which suggested historic use as an allotment from the evidence of long redundant vegetable patches, small greenhouse and old caravan, long past its sell by date.

A stock fence divided this upper 'garden' from a paddock, which sloped up to join the neighbouring fields above. The views were fantastic, all the way up to the top of Crystal Mountain, highest point on the skyline, so called because of the quartz and other minerals exposed there by the lead mine workings that were beneath it. It was so peaceful, only birdsong and the occasional sheep bleating breaking the silence.

The setting and surrounding views were wonderful; nature's stress relief therapy for free. We really liked what we were seeing, a lot of work but definite potential. We managed to arrange a proper viewing with the agent that afternoon and everything we saw made us more convinced we were meant to live here. The paddock and garden land would be more than enough for any intended self-sufficiency.

The cottage had grown like Topsy as the resident's needs changed, the only alterations being what was necessary to accommodate the growing family. Originally a single room worker's cottage with whitewashed solid stonewalls built direct onto rock and so much thicker at the bottom to spread the load, under a slate roof. The front door leading into one big room with the heart of the home, the range, in the middle. Over the years stud partitions had been put in to divide the area into two rooms, to the left a small sitting room with log burner and to the right a large kitchen diner with the original range. The lean to stores had been updated to provide a walk in pantry, shower, toilet and small utility with door onto the garden. The final addition, not yet finished inside, was an extension to the front, 'the Chapel', making another living room, a long room with log burner and windows all round giving panoramic views of the valley, French doors opening onto the garden really bringing the outside in. It was amazing to be able to see so much from one room. Upstairs was to be the compromise, as suspected it was simply a platform in the roof, which meant the eaves restricted its use and the floor was directly onto the ground floor ceiling joists so you couldn't move or eeven cough without it being heard downstairs. That apart, there were two bedrooms either side of the landing, the larger with a door to a bathroom, not ideal for overnight guests but with just the two of us, not a major issue. .

Ceiling heights throughout were an issue for Mick under the eaves, exposed beams and in doorways; I could see he was already thinking of ways to heighten the latter, the beams he would learn by painful experience to avoid. As we wandered round, despite the cobwebs and empty of furniture we felt very much at home, it felt right, a home with a heart and somewhere to feel totally content. Being able to enjoy the amazing different views of the whole valley from the windows every day would be heaven, it gave an amazing sense of being an integral part of the landscape, modern life just didn't impact on it at all.

I was dragged outside as Mick was champing at the bit to explore the old Crusher site across the lane; its industrial past in the middle of rural heaven intrigued him. Almost untouched since the mine closed in 1932 it was now some 7 acres of spoil heaps and wilderness waiting to be explored, reminding us of childhood adventures on old MOD sites. It was a wonderful mix of different levels and widely varied in its state, from native trees and conifer copse, ancient pond, spoil heaps and crushed ore plateaus, remains of old buildings all linked with dense gorse and brambles. A long-term project to make it all green again but exciting to think about and in the meantime a playground for us and paradise for Tia, no leads and no fear of encountering other dogs.

By the end of the tour we were in complete agreement. The whole place was magical, the cottage, the land, and the setting, we knew we could start to live the dream here, get back to a much simpler life without all the pressure and trappings of having material things distracting from the important things, living life rather than just planning for it and never getting to do it. We really wanted this to be our next home, who wouldn't!

We tried to be objective but were too excited at the thought of living here, yes there would be a helluva lot of physical work for the first few years but we were both fit enough to look forward to doing it. That was the whole idea, we would learn to do everything for ourselves, and the money saved from not paying others to do jobs would effectively be our earnings. If we waited another five or ten years we might not be up to the job, or find an opportunity like this. Also the housing market bubble would burst sometime and downsizing now would give us enough to come out of the sale and purchase with no mortgage and still leave a bit put by for any big purchases needed in the first few years. Me keeping on a job even on reduced hours should give us enough to pay the bills and for things we couldn't raise, make or barter for!

The distance and remoteness from family and friends was the only downside but the positive coming out of that meant that we could offer them a peaceful retreat for relaxing holidays giving us more quality time together. Much better than the hectic motorway treks we currently made to both mums still in Hampshire, most of the time spent on the road with only a few hours spent visiting.

We wanted it, apparently no one else did but as the agent pointed out we were in no position to proceed as our house wasn't even on the market and his clients were only interested in serious contenders.

We cut short our holiday, had our house on the market by the end of October and sold subject to contract by end of November, our offer on Pen y Gorof having been accepted! We worked our socks off getting ours ready for the market, chasing agents and solicitors and when things looked bad, gazumpers and chains breaking notwithstanding we overcame it all. I even managed to get a work transfer, which would let me work out of the Carmarthen office. It seemed ironic that in order to realise our dream in the remote Welsh valley I would be joining head office in London but working remotely from West Wales. Payback would be commuting the 5 hours to London regularly and stopping over whenever necessary, a small but necessary price to pay to give us a new life in the valley.

Some family and friends thought we were mad and didn't think we would go through with it. Why would anyone want to live somewhere with no mobile signal, public transport or High Street shops? Some took it as a personal affront that we wanted to move away. We did try to explain, yes it might be a mid life crisis but thoughts of mortality and carbon footprints apart this was our dream, to us living the good life would give us the satisfaction and fulfilment we were searching for. Mum was great; she was already planning her first visit and was chuffed that when I went down it would be to stay over so we would get more quality time together. Seeing everyone else would take some planning, especially once we had animals and were more tied but we didn't think it would be insurmountable, especially with good use of phones and email.

Lorries, loading and we're off!

Everything that could be boxed had been since the first week in December when we thought we would be moving. Due to problems in the chain this was delayed on a daily basis until by the 23rd we knew we wouldn't be going anywhere before Christmas and resigned ourselves to restricted festivities as the Christmas decorations were already in the store at the new house! Much time was spent planning how to get our dilapidated assortment of vehicles and all our worldly goods from central Oxfordshire to our new home in rural mid Wales as to save money we had decided to move ourselves.

Thanks to the goodwill of the sellers we had already made several ten hour round trips which had resulted in garage contents, motorbikes, jet ski (God knows when that would next be used!) and garden gear being put in the sheds and even left our pride and joy the VW Camper, loaded with more stuff in the garden. That left us with a pick up, white van and my little Peugeot. The first two were needed for the move, the Peugeot was to be left at the removals yard so that when finished Mick and I could travel back in the lorry to get it for the final journey back to Wales. First hiccup occurred when the Peugeot failed its MOT big time and couldn't be put right in time for the move. This meant the car would have to stay in the garage in Oxfordshire for collection later in the month and an extra trip for our van, and petrol, on the day so Mick had transport back after dropping off the lorry.

The removal wagons were hired by the day so to reduce costs Mick had arranged to pick the lorry up at 10a.m on the Sunday morning giving us all day to pack up our home ready for the trip to Wales as early as possible on the Monday morning, returning it to the yard in Oxford Monday evening, so avoiding another days hire. You may have realised this meant a fifteen hour round trip interspersed with the small matter of getting access to the new house and unloading the contents of our home, you may also be thinking, they are mad, hold that thought!

We set off to collect the removal lorry in good time as it was in a rural north Oxford village, which we hadn't been to before. We only got lost twice before we found a well-hidden unmade track, which led us to the yard gates. It was only ten to ten so we sat smugly waiting for the yard to be opened. When it got to 10.30 we started to get a bit twitchy. Mick climbed the gates to check if there was another way into the yard, there wasn't and there was no sign of anyone coming to open up. I tried the two phone numbers we had, both of which rang loudly in the Portakabin in the locked yard, no help there then. Mick spotted a guy feeding chickens in a nearby field and headed off to ask him if he knew the site owner at all, success, he had the mans home address, about a mile away. We drove over and managed to get a response, albeit the chaps dad who informed us that his son was at his other yard in another village some 10 miles away. He gave us the number of the yard and we phoned and confirmed with him that we would meet him there. When we finally found the other yard just after 11.15 we found that yard locked and empty! On phoning the owner's mobile he proudly told us he was now back at the original yard and would wait for us there! Rather than angry we were feeling pathetically grateful that the end appeared in sight and we would at least get a lorry today, if we didn't we were well and truly in the mire.

A quick retracing of route back to the yard found the gates open, the lorry engine running and a laid back owner keen to finish the paperwork so he could go home. Mick was given a quick briefing on driving the monster before driving home and trying to turn its length into our narrow road without taking the corner off the village green. I abandoned the car in a neighbour's drive and tried to help as multiple manoeuvres were needed to then drive the lorry into our narrow and short drive without demolishing the boundary fence, our neighbour's house wall or our bay window. Finally parked up to a round of applause and sighs of relief from the interested parties who turned out for the entertainment, we were ready to start loading.

It was already lunchtime and we were pleased when our immediate neighbour Al stayed to help us catch up, he was due to play golf in a few hours so was keen to get things done quickly and so he and Mick started loading, unfortunately not necessarily in the order we needed it packed, but we were so far behind schedule that I really didn't care. Things came to an abrupt halt when they tried to take out two large settees, which had come into the house when we had a much larger front door. It didn't matter what angle they were tilted to they wouldn't go through. Mick had to resort to taking the door off, more time lost, but problem resolved.

Just as we started packing again in earnest Al had to depart but bang on cue Dawn and Dave our pals who were helping us with the move the next day came to help out with what was left. Tia was relegated to the back garden at this point as she was going scatty trying to guard the house from all these intruders and defend any attempt to take things out by getting under feet and playing tug of war with anything she thought shouldn't be going. After what seemed an age the lorry was full, but we still had loads to go so we decided to move the lorry and start loading the vans. As Mick started to reverse out there was a horrific crunch and one side of the lorry sank into the ground. One of the driver's side wheels had broken through a manhole cover and the fully loaded lorry now had a wheel totally wedged in the hole, disaster.

After some heavy duty rocking and crunching of gears it was clear the lorry was going nowhere without heavy-duty assistance. It was late Sunday afternoon and we seemed in need of divine intervention. Taking lots of deep breaths and wandering round the garden to calm down, salvation loomed into view in the form of farmer friend Chris's tractor. I drew the short straw and went for help, which meant waking him from a well deserved afternoon nap in front of the fire. Bless him, it was the last thing he needed having been up every two hours in the night for lambing. Unceremoniously shouted awake by wife Olive he was in the mood for violent activity and within minutes had the tractor and tow chain hauling the lorry back onto solid ground and as we shouted our thanks he drove home to try and get a bit more rest before doing the sheep demanded his attention again. Luckily no damage was done to the lorry tyre, something that couldn't be said for the manhole cover. A call by Dave to a builder pal and he sourced a manhole cover for £10, which he then went and picked up for us. Lorry moved, cover replaced, we began to think someone up there liked us, better late than never.

Now dusk we went for broke to load up everything that was left, Dave's van, our panel and old pick up vans were piled high in turn as night descended. We agreed with Dawn and Dave that we would set off at 6a.m in the morning and they went home for a well-earned rest. It was now 7pm and we had yet to finish the odds and sods, clean up and find something to eat, a challenge with no cooker or food left! Out of the blue Nicola, Chris and Olives daughter in law phoned to tell me she had plated up roast dinners for us, a really kind and much appreciated gesture. I returned with laden trays, huge portions of roast dinner, jug of gravy and even bowls of apple pie and custard for dessert. A wonderful last supper, always to be remembered especially as we ate it sat on the kitchen floor.

Refuelled and ready for the final push I ran the empties back over to the farm for an emotional farewell. Spending time with Olive and Chris on the farm had sowed the seed for us wanting to have enough land to perhaps have a smallholding. It was just sad that we had to move to another country to be able to achieve it. I couldn't leave without a final visit to the stables to give a hug to my friend, Magic, Chris's horse who I mucked out every morning, he was a trusted friend, putting up with my singing and listening to my problems, in return for a good brush and daily sugar lump he always made me feel good. I was going to miss him so much. Giving him my last sugar cube and swallowing the lump in my throat I dashed back before Mick thought I had jumped ship.

We soldiered on, Mick taking down pictures we had forgotten as I mopped the kitchen floor and ran the Hoover round. Alarm set for 5a.m so we would have time to walk Tia and pack the bedding before Dawn and Dave arrived we collapsed onto the only big thing left, our mattress pulled into the front room with duvet for the night. Tia took advantage of our exhaustion and climbed on top, we were too tired to care and to be honest the extra warmth was welcome.

Escape to the new country

It didn't seem two minutes since we'd crashed out when the alarm went off. Mick took Tia for a run to tire her out so she would be content on the journey with me. We then tried to get the mattress loaded. This was not an easy feat as it was king size and pretty inflexible, made worse by the fact that we weren't exactly compatible in build with Mick at 6'4 and me 5'nothing. Getting to the lorry was exhausting enough, trying to manhandle it into a space clearly half the size it needed really didn't get the day off to a good start. After partial unloading and pushing as though our lives depended on it we were finally able to capture it behind the tailgate and lock the doors. Mental note made to stand well back when the doors got opened to avoid being flattened by a flying mattress intent on freedom.

Friends arrived, Dawn driving their van as Dave had volunteered to drive our old pick up which was piled high with the garden furniture and shed stuff, the pile was almost as big as the van itself, covered with tarpaulins roped well down to keep it all together. Mick was to head the convoy with the lorry, as he knew where he was going and was easily spotted; Dave would follow with Dawn next then me bringing up the rear. After all the trauma of the packing day we were keen for a stress free travel day, we should have realised this might not be the case when the lorry key stuck in the drivers' door. After much wriggling and borrowing of grease and WD 40 it came free and Mick finally got in the cab. We finally shut the door on our old life and set off for the new.

All went well until just outside Gloucester when the blue tarpaulins on the truck were ominously billowing like sails, trying to break free of the ropes. By the time we got to Gloucester the corners were flapping in the wind and the whole thing was in danger of taking off, after a quick mobile alert to Dave we pulled over to try and tie things down more securely. Mick unfortunately didn't have his mobile on so sailed on oblivious to us stopping. Tarpaulins tightened we set off in pursuit, it didn't take long to catch up as the road from Gloucester through the Forest of Dean was really windy with some hairpin corners which in a car were bad enough and in a loaded lorry downright dangerous. The wind picked up, playing havoc with the truck tarpaulins again and as we entered Wales bits of blue plastic were flying past at regular intervals. Mick may have no mobile to hand but was at least now using his rear view mirror and spotting the debris flying from the pick up indicated for us to pull over to try and do something with the pitiful bits of tarpaulin that were left. Dawn and I took the opportunity to let Tia and us stretch our legs, she at least got a toilet stop (Tia that is!). Dawn and Dave were really impressed we had got from Oxford to Wales in two hours; unfortunately we were only half way to our destination, Rhandirmwyn, on the west side of the Brecon Beacons National Park.

Setting off again we made good time to Brecon when with lights flashing and siren shrieking a police van came past and pulled Dave over. Mick, oblivious to the drama behind trundled on. The police van expelled six young officers who enthusiastically swarmed over and under the truck, each keen to reveal illegal immigrants or substances. Their sergeant pleased at the unexpected opportunity for an impromptu training session, Dave stood watching in bewilderment. As soon as I caught up and explained to the sarge that we were not trafficking, but simply moving house, showing him the new house particulars, he cracked a wide smile at the antics of the mad English and called off the troops, welcomed us to Wales and wished us a safe journey. Not the Welsh welcoming committee we had expected, but nonetheless memorable.

On reaching Llandovery the guys stopped for petrol for the return journey whilst Dawn and I drove on. As we went under the Heart of Wales railway bridge and started the climb up through the valley to our new home, I couldn't imagine ever taking the breathtakingly beautiful views for granted. At last we reached the sign for Rhandirmwyn closely followed by a smattering of cottages on the left and small post office and the Royal Oak pub on the right. Opposite the post office was the turning we had to take, down a steep hill to St Barnabas Church and our lane. Our lane, it sounded grand but in reality a pot holed bridleway we would be sharing with the public at large, luckily not in evidence today and all we had to negotiate was the uneven surface which slowed us to a crawl before we reached an area cleared for parking opposite the cottage overlooking the Crusher and the campsite below. Engines off, journey over at last!

First things first, of one mind Dawn and I jumped out of our respective vans and of similar mind, ran behind and squatted, not very ladylike but needs must and bliss after four hours of driving! Modesty recovered just as Mick and Dave arrived. As time was tight they started unloading the garden stuff from the truck whilst Dawn and I went back down to Llandovery to pick up the house keys, as exchange was for noon and it was now half past.

Excitedly arriving at the estate agents I was quickly brought down to earth by the receptionist who told me that she didn't think we were completing today! A bit taken aback, to say the least, I phoned our solicitor who confirmed all monies had been transferred and that the keys should be released. The estate's lady phoned the vendor's bank, but got no response, she suggested they were probably at lunch until two o clock and nothing could be done till then. Dawn could see I was about to blow a fuse and prevented an explosion by suggesting we go for a coffee whilst they sorted things out. Adding to the stress was the fact that as there was no mobile signal at the house we couldn't ring Mick to let him know what was happening, or rather what was not.

I was a nervous wreck; I'd existed on adrenalin for the last 24 hrs and really didn't need any more hiccups. We found a café on the corner opposite the agents, ordered large coffees and tried not to keep looking at the clock. It was a lovely little café with only about six tables covered in bright gingham cloths. The plates being brought out to the other tables having lunch were piled high and the smells of battered fish and smoked ham were tempting, but despite the distraction my mind was all too aware of the fact that we had four vehicles to unload before it got dark and we were only 4 hours away from that happening, plus the small matter of another six hour round trip to return the lorry and get back home before our day was over.

At half one I could wait no longer and so we returned to the agents to find no one had heard anything yet and so sat dejectedly on the windowsill to wait. Every time the phone rang my heart leapt but each time it was nothing to do with our sale. The wait did help me calm down, if we got nowhere today it would happen tomorrow and I was resigning myself to a night in the removals van, another £100 for an extra days hire and losing Dawn and Dave's help as they had to return this evening. Positive thinking obviously did the trick; at five past two the call came giving the all clear for us to have the keys. Hugs all round; stress level receded from the red, back to the lads!

Conscious of the time I drove back up the valley rather manically; Dawn gripping the seat, concerned at how close to the edge of the drop to the river I was going. I was oblivious, smiling from ear to ear, the house was ours, and we were going to move in, all was well with the world. On arrival Mick and Dave were understandably peeved at the wait they had had. Having unloaded as much as they could, walking the land several times and having had to take advantage of the rather dubious porta potty in the dilapidated 1950s caravan left in the top garden, they were in no mood for hearing our story, just itching to get unloaded and on the road as soon as possible.

The next four hours passed in a blur, allocating everything to kitchen, bedrooms, sitting room, and sheds as we unloaded everything as quick as we could, no time for unpacking or assembling anything. Luckily the two big settees fitted in the French doors to the sitting room but as there was a 2ft drop to ground level it was almost as awkward trying to manhandle them into our new home as it was getting them out of the old, Dave put his knee out in the process, hopefully the last casualty of the day. It was getting dark now as the lads unloaded the final boxes.

Getting some sort of bed arranged became a priority as by the time we had returned the lorry to Oxfordshire and driven back again we would be fit for nothing. Too late to assemble the frame Dawn and I manhandled two mattresses one atop the other on the floor in the bedroom, it was really cold already and with no heating it was fair to say it would get even colder by the time we finally got to bed so we threw on top every duvet, and blanket we could find. The result was a giant nest of jumble. Resisting the temptation to burrow in we rejoined the lads to try and finish unloading before we lost the light completely.

By 5.30 it was pitch black, no moon or stars yet to lighten the sky, the final box was in and we had one last thing to do before we got back on the road again. Perched on boxes in the kitchen, bereft of any heating, huddled in our coats we opened a bottle of champagne to toast our achievement and our new home, drank out of our flask mugs, by the light of the lorry headlights! By six we reformed the convoy for the return journey. Dawn and Dave in their van, followed by Mick in the lorry, then me in our white van with Tia for company. In total darkness with only headlights and taillights visible we edged our way back down the valley.

The journey seemed never ending, adrenalin had definitely run out and exhaustion was seeping in but we safely reached

Oxfordshire and Dawn and Dave sounded their horn as they continued home whilst we pulled into a garage to fill up tanks and buy sandwiches and pop to keep us awake for the final leg back to Wales. Lorry safely left at the deserted yard Mick swapped seats with me and we hit the road again. I prattled on about nothing to keep him awake, until he told me to shut up as it was having the reverse effect! The further we got the less traffic we encountered and it felt like we were trapped in the Twilight Zone, driving for evermore. For the final stretch from Brecon to Rhandirmwyn Mick was on autopilot and all credit to him for keeping awake and the van not only on the road, but also in the right direction. We finally arrived back at 1a.m, staggered upstairs and burrowed under the bedding nest, quickly joined by Tia whose cold snout was no comfort but we were too tired to push her out. We could finally relax; we looked up at the stars glittering through the roof lights, listened to the owls calling and felt all the stresses of the day melt away. Smiling like cats that'd got the cream we fell asleep as soon as our heads hit the pillows.

Reality bites

Not sure if it was being utterly exhausted or sleeping on two mattresses under three duvets and every blanket we owned but we slept like logs and were loathe to move on waking as we were so warm and cosy. Poking our noses out of our nest it was quickly clear it was blooming freezing everywhere else. Tia, already up and exploring new smells let us know it was time for her to go out by trying to unearth us with her snout which was icy, blankets flying in all directions and running out of places to hide I reached out for the pile of clothes dropped next to the bed in my haste to get in and quickly pulled them on to try and mitigate the shock of leaving the warm covers. I needn't have bothered, I forgot we had no hot water and the subsequent cold splash was another shock to the system, but raising my head to look out the window took my breath away more than the cold water. It was beautiful, looking up over the neighbouring stables and fields to the top of Crystal Mountain, capped with snow atop a forest of conifers.

Whilst I viewed the surround Mick located the switch for the immersion so we would at least get hot water until we could arrange for the oil tank to be filled and get the range going, as it not only cooked but also provided heat and hot water. The gas hob alongside was bereft of gas bottle so we were restricted to toast for breakfast before we took Tia for a walk around the garden and paddock, collecting fallen wood to light the two wood burners which were in each of the sitting rooms and would, chimneys being clear permitting, take the edge off of the cold and begin to air out the house.

As well as no mobile signal there was also no aerial reception, phone or Internet connection, we were completely without any way of contacting the outside world to get the services we needed. We had our hopes raised that at least we would have TV due to the small Sky dish on the side of the porch, but on closer inspection Mick noticed the transmitter had gone AWOL. Digging out all the phone numbers we needed we drove the seven miles down the valley to Llandovery where we could get a mobile signal and spent a pleasant (not!), hour sat in a Somerfield car park organising telephone connection and an oil supply. Despite the frustration of automated services and doubling the mobile bill we managed to arrange dates for both. A quick trip round the shop for food essentials and helpful advice from the checkout girl saw us driving to the nearby village of Llandeilo to a TV shop to arrange installation of a working satellite dish for us the following week. Mission accomplished and armed with supplies we headed home, looking forward to camping out until we were connected to the outside world again.

Stopping at the village post office/shop we bought a gas bottle for the hob and introduced ourselves to the postmaster and his wife who were the font of all knowledge for all things local, really friendly and happy to help newcomers settle in. It was a nice feeling to know they would look out for us and we happily set off down the hill to 'home.'

The first week passed in a blur of cleaning, making homeless legions of daddy longlegs, unloading boxes and finding homes for everything. We had set up camp in the smaller sitting room, as it was easier to heat. During the day Mick collected enough wood to fire up the log burner and we fought Tia for space on the bed settee. She was quite put out as prior to moving she always slept on it. We compromised and shared, letting her settle in the middle, grateful for the extra warmth. It took us a while to adjust to not having the telly but then we really found it relaxing, just sitting in peace and quiet, rather than fighting for control of the remote and getting cross at the rubbish that was on. Instead we were surrounded by books such as Paul Heiney's 'Home Farm – A Practical Guide To The Good Life' and similar worthy tomes, helping us to see how our wish list of what we would like to do balanced against the practicalities of what our land would enable us to do. For light relief we watched nature's TV out of the window, watching day turn to night, the new moon and stars slowly coming out and listening to the late blackbird song followed by owl calls, interspersed with odd shrieks, barks and noises from animals we had yet to identify, before total silence fell. Definitely a culture changes from the ever-present streetlights, traffic and people noise of our previous life. We quickly adapted to the new routine, the combination of fresh air, tiredness and no TV meant we were in bed before 9.30, and as a consequence up bright and early when the early morning bird choir chivvied us to get up and enjoy the new day.

Rhandirmwyn seemed to have its own unique weather system; contrary to forecasts within an hour we could experience extreme rain, sun, and high winds in quick succession. We took locals advice, which was to avoid making plans to do things by dates and instead be led by the weather. If it rained do indoor jobs, if not make the most of getting things done outside. This ensured things always got done, just not necessarily when you thought they would. It took us some time to get our heads round this as in the past we set days for doing certain things and if weather stopped us we simply sat indoors watching TV or went shopping. No such luxury when you are miles from anywhere and have no TV. We quickly realised when not doing the jobs we would be sourcing and buying everything we needed in advance so no matter what the weather we would be able to get on with something. Glossy clothes and car mags were replaced with Thompson & Morgan seed catalogues, Farmers weekly and Smallholder monthly. There's got to be a pun in there somewhere, how come farmers do it once a week but smallholders only once a month? We found out the answer by trial and error – a farmer knows exactly what to do and does it on a weekly basis, a smallholder takes a week to decide what they think they want to do, a week to research it, a week to realise its not achievable and a week to find out from the farmer the right way to do it!

Home on the range & unwanted guests

The blackened range in the kitchen was a wonderful feature and in the past had provided all the essentials for the cottage, hot water, heat and cooking. Mick was determined to restore it to former glory and I came home to a kitchen covered with its dismembered parts and Mick sat in the middle looking like a coal miner just off shift. A week later after a complete strip down and rebuild followed by doing the same with the pipework both to the oil tank and to the water tanks he was satisfied it could be safely fired up. The oil tank was now full and so with an improvised drum roll from me on the kitchen table Mick turned it on and lit the burner, no explosion or leaks, the cottage had its heart pumping again and it slowly came back to life.

The first benefit was heat radiating out in all directions. Pre firing up upstairs was like an icebox, now as you reached the landing the heat wrapped round you like a welcoming blanket. It explained why no radiators were needed in our bedroom. The range was top of the shop in 1950 and from its battle scars had seen heavy service for the majority of its life. As the weeks went by I was impressed with just how many and varied the services it provided were, this old piece of iron really was the heart of the home. It had a rack over the top, which made excellent clothes drier (or wine fermenter!), and a bar in front that meant towels and tea towels were always dry and well aired. No more need for clothes line or a tumble drier, washing went straight from washer to clothes horse around the range for the night and was ready for the airing cupboard the next day, likewise wet weather gear was always quickly dried, an essential given our wet micro climate.

When the heavy hotplate lid was lifted, a two handed job, it could accommodate 3 saucepans, the plate varying from boiling to simmering gently, dependant on which end you placed them. The area round the hotplate kept a constant warmth making it ideal for keeping food, mulled wine or gloves warm, or defrosting bread or anything else needed in haste from the freezer. The oven itself was really big and basic, no confusing numbers just a simple temperature gauge showing cold, medium or hot. An added bonus was that there were no stainless or enamel surfaces needing attention, everything just burnt off, my kind of cleaning! Underneath was a warming compartment ideal for keeping food hot until needed or warming everything from plates to resuscitating baby animals! All this as well as heating the water and radiators to the hottest temperature we'd experienced. The previous owners had left a battered box of weird looking cast iron bits, which apparently enabled the range to be converted back to wood burning. Mick quite liked the option, especially as oil prices were creeping steadily up, but not to be tried until we had rebuilt and filled the wood shed.

The downside of the range having so many uses was that it took a long while to learn how to use it to best effect. Using a lot of hot water reduced the oven heat, so having hot baths whilst waiting on roast potatoes to brown or cakes to rise was a recipe for disaster. On the other hand if you didn't use the hot water and kept the oven at high temperature the water boiled in the pipes and the upstairs became a sauna, fine during the winter but not conducive to a good nights sleep in the summer. Getting the heat back up on the oven took quite a while so after a few abortive meals with anaemic sausages and flat sponges I learnt to adapt and work to its pace rather than mine. At its hottest in the morning I did all my baking, in the evening as temperature had dropped after baths I started things off on the gas hob, finishing them in the oven or on the hotplate.

With a few more tweaks to its inner workings the heat became more stable and with the addition of the hotplates on top of the two sitting room wood burners I was intent on economising by producing food without resorting to using the gas hob or microwave. Added bonuses were the resulting physical work out from juggling pots and pans between heat sources in the different rooms and the look of bemusement on visitor's faces as I raced from one end of the cottage to the other. It was surprising how keen Mick and guests were to help; there was definitely something about cooking outside the kitchen that made people want to join in, fine by me!

Laid in bed warm and content enjoying the stillness of the night we became aware we were not alone in enjoying the home comforts. Persistent scrabbling and movement around the roof lining and eaves cupboards let us know that at best mice, or at worst squirrels or rats, were also enjoying respite from the cold outside. Inspection of the loft hatch and wardrobes revealed it was mice, who weren't fussy about toilet etiquette and had made an even bigger mess having destroyed the insides of my furry slipper boots. The next night humane traps with tasty chocolate duly placed we looked forward to a good nights sleep, how naïve. Every half hour between midnight and 2 a.m the traps were rattled frantically by trapped mice trying to force their way out, each time I donned dressing gown and wellies, armed myself with a torch and took the trap down to the bottom of the garden where I let the spunky little fellas out to find a new home. By the third night and 12 empties later I was convinced it was the same ones following me back in, if so I could appreciate their persistence, though if not we were on the verge of an invasion. As some lights were beginning to flicker we guessed the electric cables were beginning to prove tasty nibbles and no matter how cute the culprits looked it was now them or us so hardier deterrents were put down and within four days there was no sign of anything living indoors other than Mick, Tia and me. Though the width of the solid walls and gaps under the eaves gave easy access to the intrepid beasties and we would have to find ways to close all access before next winter.

While the weather was still awful Mick set to bringing the inside of the cottage to a more lived in state. Three weeks and buckets of emulsion later he had completely repainted every single wall and ceiling with fresh brilliant white, even Tia was sporting fetching white streaks in her tail. The downside to the move was that I was now travelling to London every week for work and as it was a 10 hour round trip had to stay up for two nights. The pay back was coming home to such a contrast and seeing how much the cottage had changed in such a short time. The place was beginning to feel like our home. The sky dish had been put up and the TV was now working, we even had a dial up Internet connection. Now we could source what we needed and pay for everything online, reducing long road trips and phone bills, getting things delivered or ensuring when we had to go out we didn't get lost and got what we needed.

Boys Toys (or essential kit for the smallholder!!)

During another wet spell spent indoors Mick worked out what mechanical help he would need to do the outside jobs to achieve secure fencing over the widely varying levels and types of surface, from the bottom of the Crusher across the lane and onto the top of the paddock. First on his wish list of big boys toys was a JCB for heavy-duty jobs, followed by a tractor for general workhorse and a quad bike for everything in-between, from pulling small loads to carrying bales in awkward places. Hours were then spent with local trades papers and on the computer trying to find the elusive bargain, one that was in working order, easy to get spares, close to home and cheap.

  The quad was the first arrival, four wheels of off road fun and games, which we both got familiar with down in the Crusher which had quickly become our very own adventure playground. It had so many places to explore, from boggy old ponds to undulating spoil heaps criss crossed with rabbit warrens, small copses and high-banked conifer woodland. My turn on the bike involved sedately pottering around on the level, turning in very wide circles, Mick shouting instructions in the middle trying to get me to speed up enough to be able to go up the slopes. In complete contrast Mick standing tall and revving at speed raced up the spoil heaps, flying through the air across the tops before cornering on two wheels to race off in another direction, his years of endurance bike racing coming into play. Fun over we moved on to learning how to work the quad with a trailer attached. No problem for Mick his patience started to wear thin as he showed me for the tenth time how to reverse with a loaded trailer on the back. Going forward great, going backwards without trailer not bad, going backwards with trailer, hello ditch. After yet another aborted attempt I decided to quit before we fell out big time and by mutual agreement it was decided Mick would be driving anything that involved a trailer going backwards and I was relegated to wingman.

  When arranging house insurance we were told we needed additional cover for all land in our ownership to prevent being sued by anyone suffering an accident on it. The Crusher site which wasn't fenced from the lane, with all the different spoil heaps, bore holes and wild areas was an accident waiting to happen. To get cover we had to fence it off. Now we had the quad to make the job easier Mick worked out what was needed and placed our first big order with our local builders yard. Two days later the sound of a lorry reversing down the lane heralded the arrival of bundle after bundle of fence posts, rolls of stock fencing and topping wire.

Quad duly loaded with fencing materials, shovel and lump hammer Mick started off enthusiastically on the first posthole. It was a big enough job as the lane was so long, but made a whole lot worse by the differing levels of the banks along the boundary. The rocky ground fought back as Mick tried to get a decent depth to the hole. I tried to help as much as possible, steadying posts, passing tools and clearing patches of undergrowth ahead of hole digging. What I lacked in the strength front I made up for with enthusiasm. The satisfaction of seeing the results at the end of the day followed by the wonderful completely relaxed feeling after easing aching bodies with hot baths and a deep uninterrupted nights sleep was a complete contrast to pre move fretting over unresolved office issues and suffering insomnia as a result.

Two days later the full length of the lane was completed with all fence posts finally knocked home and we celebrated with our first meal at the local pub The Royal Oak at the top of the hill. An enormous log fire welcomed us, as did everyone in there. Real ales flowed and the local Welsh Black beef curry special was a great choice. As the night wore on we noticed everyone who came in had torches and on leaving much later realised why. The minute the pub was behind us there was nothing to light the path back down the hill, not a star in the sky or even a half decent moon. We set off into the total darkness, full of good spirits, literally! By the time we were halfway down we were completely disorientated, we knew there were ditches on either side and hoped we were in the middle of the narrow road but by the change in surface underfoot could tell we were wandering. I was in front and every time I looked behind Mick was on a different side of the lane, or was that me wandering? Weaving from one side to the other we must have looked ridiculous, gingerly testing each footstep and giggling hysterically as we went. As we rounded a corner a single light opposite St Barnabas Church gave us a beacon to head for and we picked the pace up. Reaching the light we were then faced by the challenge of heading off into the pitch black again along our lane. We discovered that going from new fence post to post kept us on a more or less straight line, well at least until I went in the wrong direction off one post, tripping on tree roots and laying helpless with laughter on my back as Mick wandered round playing Blind Man's Buff trying to find me and get me upright. Finally on the home stretch, arm in arm for mutual support the cottage light hove into view, leading us home. Never again would we venture out without a light to guide us home! The next morning I lined up three torches next to the front door to remind us of our folly.

If we thought putting the fence posts up was the hard part we were quickly proved wrong when trying to tighten and fasten the stock fencing and topping wire along them, it had a life of its own, recoiling back on itself as fast as it was unraveled. Much cursing, aching backs and skinned knuckles later the final piece was hammered in place. It was easy to see how much improved Mick's skill in fence making had got by seeing how by the end the fence posts were solid and the fence taut rather than sagging dolefully between wobbly posts which had been the case when we started. The addition of three field gates to different parts of the Crusher completed the job.

We felt proud of the result, especially when a neighbour out walking stopped to compliment us on the improvement, though he did rather spoil it by asking why we had put the stock wire on the wrong way up? How were we to know the first row of wire had smaller holes at the bottom to stop rabbits and similar small invaders coming through? Why couldn't he have come past and noticed just as we started?! Not that it made any difference as far as the lane fencing was concerned but it was a lesson learned for when we came to do the vegetable patch.

Planning the plot

First priority outside as the weather improved was to discover what was in the gardens and put into practice the results of our deliberations as to what was going where. First we wanted space for an orchard, vegetable patch and animal enclosures. It made sense that any working areas should be away from the lane that was open to walkers and so Mick set to clearing the rear garden alongside the paddock that was to house the veg patch and orchard. It was clear from old posts and different surfaces that over the years piecemeal cultivated patches had been made but were now totally redundant so Mick set to reclaiming anything he could for future use and making a bonfire of anything he couldn't. The worse job was trying to get old carpets up which were not rotting down but were well trapped by the persistent nettle, buttercup and dock roots.

Our thoughts then turned to making best use of the paddock. We were definitely in favour of keeping chickens, fresh eggs collected each day would be a real treat. Originally we had intended to let local farmers put sheep on the rest of the paddock just to keep the grass down but having chatted to a local farmer, Mick was persuaded that if we were going to have livestock on the land it should be our own. Visions of River Cottage and Jamie's Farm sprung to mind with much loved animals, well fed and kept in as natural environment as possible throughout their lives and as stress free as possible when their time was up.

To have the best of both worlds we decided we would keep resident mums who would be part of the family letting them have offspring each year who would have a happy childhood before departing when they reached the obnoxious teenage stage, reappearing as meat packs to make us self sufficient in meat. It was one thing to feed and care for animals but to make it viable we needed to breed and sell the product as well without getting too attached, and there lies the rub. Farm friend looked over the paddock and suggested it would sustain not only the chicken run but also a pig enclosure and half a dozen sheep. The intention would be for 6 chickens to provide enough eggs for us, a sow, that would have a litter each year, and 4-6 ewes, which would produce lambs each year. This would give us a continuous source of eggs, pork and lamb with any extra being bartered with friends or sold locally. We knew it wouldn't make us rich but hopefully it would cover the cost of feed and keep of the animals, plus more importantly we could stop buying meat and feeling guilty about where it had come from and how it had got there. Rainy days gave us a lot of time to talk it through and Mick worked out where the hen house and pigsty would go together with runs for them all, before making yet more lists of things needed to build it all.

After another rainy afternoon going through old farming magazines Mick triumphantly produced a battered advert ringed in red, an old JCB, in budget, in Abergavenny was still available and he was going to look at it the next day. By the end of the week he was playing Bob the Builder in the Crusher, happy as a pig in muck swinging the bucket arm into a heap and scooping large amounts before swiveling the JCB round and depositing the spoil at the bottom of the track up to the lane. He could then use the front-loading scoop at ground level to push it along filling the ruts and rolling them firm in one operation. It was amazing how effective it was. The JCB was to live in the bottom of the Crusher as it certainly had space for it, was out of sight and ready for action whenever Mick needed it. The long-term aim was to bring the Crusher back to green fields and woodland but that was very obviously a long way off, even with the JCB, it would be like using a teaspoon to empty a sandpit. Still, even with the small inroads we had made we could see what could be achieved and with much more hard manual labour to come this was light relief for Mick.

A taste of the country

Walking Tia along the lanes I noticed the Elderflower was in full bloom in a number of places in the hedgerows and got excited at the prospect of turning it to wine. Elderflower is one of my favourites, as good as any Chardonnay and I had been happy to pay for it in the past. I was really pleased to find five trees close to home that would ensure I could build up my own stocks. All I needed to do was remember where they were, next morning armed with carrier bags, Tia had to amuse herself while I climbed in and out of the hedge filling the bags as I went with the large lacy white flower heads, they smelt wonderful and I soon had two carrier bags full. Now all I had to do was find the wine making bits and bobs, which were somewhere in the garage loft. What better way to spend a rainy afternoon? Demi johns and buckets located I was ready to start. The range not only heated the water at the beginning of the process but would also finish the operation with the rising heat encouraging fermentation of the resulting demijohns, which would be placed on the rack above. A good-looking talking point for visitors and so much better than being hidden in an airing cupboard.

Country wines are so easy to make, needing no expensive kit just a plastic bucket, a saucepan big enough to hold eight pints of water, demijohns, old wine bottles, corks and a glass! 6 bottles cost around £3 so you can see the attraction. My carrier bags of elderflowers were quickly converted to two demijohns bubbling away nicely.

Elderflower wine recipe

1 pint Elderflowers (no stalks, pushed down but still springy), 3lb sugar, 6pts boiling water, 1 lemon & 1 orange rinds and juice, ½ cup cold strong tea, 1 campden tablet, Wine yeast, yeast nutrient.

Put Elderflowers, Lemon & Orange rinds, juice and tea in a plastic bucket and stir in boiling water, stir well cover and leave in warm place for 4 days. Strain liquid into saucepan and bring to the boil. Put sugar in clean plastic bucket and pour over liquid, stir to dissolve and when cool add crushed campden tablet, 24 hours later add the yeast and nutrient, cover and leave for 6 days somewhere warm stirring daily. Transfer to demijohn with airlock to continue fermentation. Once finished if clear bottle or rack into another demijohn and leave until clear. Store on a cold floor, the back of the pantry, garage or garden shed is a good place to forget about them until they are ready to drink in 6 months time.

All country wines taste better the longer they are left so if you don't like the taste don't write if off just leave it for another month and try again.

As the ground dried Mick's attention turned to the paddock, which would be the centre of the smallholding. It was two and a half acres and well drained as it sloped down from our boundary with our neighbour's fields to a level adjoining the veg garden. Unfortunately as the grass had been untouched for some 4 years areas of bracken and reed grass had taken strong hold and the areas of remaining grass were long and matted preventing new growth from coming through. The stock fencing was also long past its sell by date in places so before we could even consider having livestock Mick's first task was to develop his fencing skills further spending days clearing the debris, patching the wire, banging in old posts and replacing those which splintered on contact.

Returning from London Mick informed me he had a temporary solution to the paddock grass problem in the form of a pony called Minstrel who would be arriving the next day. My initial concern that he was suggesting we turn French and produce horse meat was put to rest when Mick explained the pony belonged to Nerys, a neighbour who just needed temporary grazing and it would hopefully make some improvement to the grass, chomping it down and fertilizing it at the same time. Minstrel was a sweetheart and quickly settled in, Tia doing her best to make her welcome by licking her face every time she lowered her head over the fence and me by feeding her with carrots, which quickly cemented our friendship. Nerys came twice a day to feed and check on her and kindly brought much appreciated jars of her home made runner bean chutney, Branston fan Mick loved it and luckily Nerys didn't mind sharing the recipe, a good incentive to get the veg patch up and running so I had a good harvest of runner beans to make my own.

Runner Bean Pickle recipe:
When I found myself with a glut I found substituting Turmeric with Garam Marsala, producing an excellent variation

tasting just like mango chutney, two excellent preserves from one humble bean and I now ensure I have enough to make copious amounts of both to provide year round pickle and chutney. Superb with cheese, curries and any meat dishes.

    2lbs runner beans, stringed and roughly chopped
    1&1/2 lbs onions, chopped
    1 teaspoon dried mustard
    3 tablespoons cornflour
    1 ½ pts vinegar
    1 ½ tablespoons tumeric(pickle) or Garam Marsala (chutney)
    Pinch of salt.

Cook beans in salted water until tender, strain. Cook onions in ½ pint vinegar until tender then add beans and another ½ pint of vinegar, cook for 15 minutes. Add sugar. Mix cornflour, spice and mustard with remaining ½ pint vinegar, stir into beans and onions. Bring to boil and simmer for 10 minutes. Remember it will thicken further on cooling, pot and store. Whilst really tasty after a month it becomes even tastier the longer it is stored and my aim is for it to last us until the next harvest the following August. Gardener friends are happy to offload surplus beans in return for a jar of pickle for Christmas.

Tree taming

The rear of the cottage was close to the bank of an old pond originally made for the lead mine and used to drive the waterwheel for the Crusher machinery to extract lead whilst doubling up as a communal baths for the miners before going home. Long dry and in need of repuddling if it was ever to hold water again the eight foot high bank ran along the full length of the cottage and was topped by 5 very old, very large and very rotten trees. The enormous crown of branches filled the sky above the cottage and hung ominously over the velux roof lights of the bedrooms and landing. The survey for our purchase informed us that they should be attended to as a first priority. Whenever it rained the branches seemed to bat the drops into the windows with the force of gatling gunfire and when the wind blew down the valley I would lay awake waiting for branches to fall and trying to remember where the buildings insurance paperwork was stashed.

Another enormous oak tree towered over the corner of the garden and paddock. Although it looked impressive it was very dead and the size of the branches, which were blown off with increasing regularity, was causing considerable mayhem. An enormous cracking noise at 2a.m one morning saw one such branch bury the picnic bench beneath it right up to its tabletop. Realising the damage that could be done to the cottage if the trees there followed suit Mick asked a farmer friend if he knew anyone who would take them down for us. Said farmer volunteered to fell them in return for the wood and we willingly took up the offer, peace of mind and no money to spend, our kind of deal.

Two months later we were becoming wise to the fact that although it would get done it would be in rural time, which like the weather was quite unpredictable. Finally he arrived armed with enormous chainsaws, tractor, old chains and a pal to help. The cottage trees were going to be done, leaving the paddock oak for another day. The plan being to chain each tree to the tractor manned by farmers pal, which would stay, pointed up the lane ready to pull the trees away from the house once farmer cut a wedge out of the base of the trunk big enough to let them topple over. Ropes were employed as a back up to the chains and were to be manned by Mick.

I had by now managed to qualify for homeworking reducing my London trips to twice a month so as they began I naively started working in my 'office', more commonly known as the landing, one ear tuned to the continuous drone of the chainsaw. Sudden silence followed by Mick yelling at me to get Tia and myself out of the house brought me to my feet and to the window. The first and biggest tree was in danger of falling the wrong way onto the roof. I flew down the stairs and out to the sheds at the bottom of the garden, only then turning back to look at the enormous tree swaying ominously above the cottage. The chain had snapped and Mick was fighting to keep the ropes taut to prevent the trunk from twisting back to the cottage whilst another chain was fixed so the tractor could pull it to safety. In slow motion the trunk swaying ominously closer to the chimney stack, only to be stopped just as the branches were brushing the roof by the tractor taking up the slack of the new chain and driving up the lane, pulling the tree in the right direction safely away from our home. One minute the enormous crown of branches filled the skyline, then with an earsplitting crack, it disappeared, revealing a wonderful view up the valley to the peaks beyond. Cheers from behind the cottage followed by Mick coming round for three well earned coffees gave me the confidence to go back in whilst the chaps, testosterone levels at their highest, set to the remaining trees with gusto. By mid afternoon all were felled without further mishap.

At the end of the day two of the trunks had been cut up, the remainder lay stretched out across the old pond. It really was a rotten sight and I mean that literally, any doubts on whether felling was the right thing to do were dispelled when we saw how rotten the timber was, no candidates for ending up as bespoke bits of furniture from this lot. Large broken lifeless limbs were scattered everywhere, not a decent growing part in sight. To Mick, a real fire and chainsaw enthusiast it was Christmas come early; there would be no problem with filling the woodshed this year, or even next!

That night laying looking up through the roof lights I was amazed at the difference, before odd stars would flash through the black branches but now the manically swaying branches were replaced by an uninterrupted magical array of glittering stars. Despite the really heavy winds the stars, unlike the tree branches remained constant and reassuring. I fell into a contented sleep safe in the knowledge the roof would be intact in the morning.

Farmer's jobs left him no time to cut up any more of the big trunks so after a fortnight of waiting Mick invested in a bigger chainsaw and set to himself, farmer returning to collect his due just as Mick had finished. That left all the remaining branches to be cut for firewood to go in our wood shed and the brash to be burnt in a bonfire, which lasted almost a week. What a great way to end each day, joining Mick with a brew, sitting on upturned logs, the intense heat scorching our faces as we watched the fire dancing and sparking high in the sky, lighting the darkness. The icing on the cake was a filled to bursting woodshed and veg patch richly dug with wood ash. Recycling at its best.

A load of bullocks

A chance meeting in the lane introduced us to Ab the Farm Manager of our neighbours, Coleg Elidyr, who was really welcoming and pleased to advise and help us with setting up the smallholding. He suggested the current state of the paddock would take more than the pony grazing or even sheep to bring it back to productive use without a complete overhaul. Relating a well known farmer's saying: A pig will starve a sheep, a sheep will starve a cow, which roughly translated means cattle like long grass as they pull it, sheep munch it too short for cows, pigs destroy it completely by rooting it up and so starve the sheep.

Because of the overgrown state of our grass two options were suggested, the first involved a lot of machinery for cutting, harrowing, rolling etc which would be costly, time consuming and difficult to arrange with the sloping nature of the paddock, our limited resources and knowledge. The second, preferred, and more user-friendly option was to borrow 20 of Ab's Welsh black bullocks that would do the same job within two weeks and spare the College's grass whilst they were with us. As the growing season was in full swing Nerys was happy to take Minstrel home to her own paddock so that we could crack on with getting the cattle in. We bid our first new animal friend a fond farewell and looked forward to the arrival of the cattle.

Our lane joined the Coleg field lane, which led up to the farm and campus. Ab and his student helpers simply drove the cattle from their existing field along the lane to ours. It was a first for us walking alongside as the bullocks trotted through the gate and set about boisterously exploring the paddock, like a rugby squad charging a target before scrumming down to get the tastiest bit. The students had a great sense of fun and were happy to chat with us on the joys of rural living and how they enjoyed working with the animals and doing other craftwork as well as normal studies. The whole set up seemed like a great extended family. Due to behavioral problems the students were full time residents at the Coleg (Welsh for college) living in houses around the grounds, each house with houseparents and helpers looking after them, it was a real home from home and they obviously loved the lifestyle and sense of community, I was quite envious!

Ab warned us that whilst totally good natured the bullocks

were blooming strong and so we should always have an eye to what they were doing and not put ourselves in a position to be jostled or knocked over. Wise words, the bullocks were so curious, especially if Tia was about and a little bit too enthusiastic in their keenness to get close for a sniff they were quite intimidating, stampeding across the field towards her, she quickly learnt to make a beeline for the gates and we got adept at waving them off if they got too close to us. Safely on the other side of the fence though we happily stroked muzzles and scratched ears as they jostled to get close and make friends.

Watching from the window the next morning we were surprised at how organised they were in working over the paddock. They lined themselves up, evenly spaced across one end, and in unison advanced in a straight line as they grazed before getting together for some rough housing and rest before resuming position and continuing the advance. Within two days we could definitely see where they had been and the improvement to the ground. The constant trampling was evening out the worst of the bumps, grazing producing an even cut and muck spreading on the result improving the grass quality. 20 cattle doing the job of four machines and humans, I know what I preferred to watch.

All too soon the bullocks had grazed the paddock as far as they could and were spending longer trampling round, which with the return of wet weather meant it was time for them to go and for us to get sheep to continue the maintenance. Ab was right, bang on two weeks after arrival we bid them a fond farewell and they trotted off back down the lane to pastures new.

In between showers Mick fenced and railed the pig and hen run from part of the paddock alongside the veg garden. Getting posts in was the biggest problem as it seemed no matter which position was chosen to knock them in two foot down there would be the proverbial rock and hard place beyond which the thing wouldn't go. Despite this Mick managed to get them in as far as possible to support the stock fencing and barbed wire he stretched across them. We had no specialist tools for the job and as with the lane, it was a definite learning curve trying to get the fencing taut. Necessity being the mother of invention saw Mick using the garden fork to stretch the wire as far as possible around the intended post until taut and then capturing it by hammering home the fence staples.

Recruited to do the simple task of knocking the staples home whilst Mick strained to get the wire taut was beyond me, I missed the staples; hit the post, Micks hand, my hand and anything other than the target. On the rare occasions I did make contact with the staple I lacked the strength to make any impact on the beggar. Mick sacked me and I was relegated to fetching, carrying and tidying up. The plan was for the chicken run to be at the top end closest to the house (where the offending bench killing tree had yet to be taken down), pigpen alongside with access from the garden into the paddock. We hoped to get the chickens up and running then buy the sheep and lastly the pig. The paddock grass was in need of grazing to keep it in good order so we needed to get sheep as soon as possible. Farmer friend had promised that for a reasonable price he could provide all the stock we would need.

Unfortunately this was not to be as farmer friend disappeared for a while following an unfortunate incident involving drink, a tractor and attempted demolition of static caravans. Consequently we needed to rethink sheep providers and also how we were going to deal with felling the unsafe paddock oak. As the tree would threaten our first choice of site for the proposed chicken run Mick simply decided to relocate the site to the other end of the pig pen so he could at least complete the chicken part of our self sufficiency plan.

We wanted a 'one stop shop' building for the chickens, lots of space and light, room to increase flock number, easy access for cleaning and room for feed/bedding storage. Checking the Internet and local ads we were amazed at the cost of really small housing and the number of 'essential additions' which pushed the price up to way over that of a decent sized shed. A quick look in the Screwfix catalogue proved this very much the case and so a 6 ft x 8 ft timber and felt shed with double front doors and side windows was duly ordered with delivery promised within 7 days.

Mick set about levelling a base for the chicken hut, cutting out the turf and levelling with scalpings. Screwfix delivered as promised and Mick set to creosoting all the timber sections in the workshop next to the house during a rainy couple of days which prevented fieldwork.. I love the smell of creosote, good job really as the smell came straight through the chimney vent wafting throughout the house, making even the ironing pile smell of it.

Carrying the finished sections from the workshop round to

the base was a challenge, our disparate heights ill matched for carrying large items, luckily the path around the cottage was equally uneven and we struck quite a good balance. Within a couple of hours we proudly surveyed the new chicken house, our first completed outbuilding, fitted with bespoke luxury innovations, using a heavy duty builders plastic lining for the floor for easy cleaning and replacing the side window with narrow mesh to ensure a good air flow to the benefit of the birds, and us when mucking out. The final addition being a purpose built wooden 'ladder' raised at the back of the shed to provide staggered nesting perches. The side under the window was to be the egg laying area and two large round logs would keep the nesting boxes clear of the floor. All that was now missing was the nesting boxes and chickens to fill them.

In-between trying to find other local sheep for sale Mick turned his attention to the now growing paddock grass. It was looking really good following the makeover by the cattle but was starting to get above sheep munching levels again. The sun had come through and having had no rain for a week or two the grass growth accelerated. Two leads for getting sheep had proven abortive and the odd strays finding their way in were only tickling the top. It was beginning to look like we would have to give in and pay someone to cut it, but not if Mick had anything to do with it.

I was amazed to come home from work to find him in the paddock with our petrol push mower and cans of petrol lined up along the fence. Not for him the easy option of paying to get the job done, or even hiring a sit on mower. Starting from the outside and working in Mick valiantly set off, stopping it seemed every ten foot to dislodge the clumps of matted grass, stones and sticks and restart, tormented by the sight of sheep in neighbouring fields. Like the Duracell Bunny he would not stop despite blisters, cuts from flying debris and continual servicing of the mower he kept on, and on, and on, only stopping when he lost the light. Three days later it was done, the final 2ft square of uncut mess celebrated with a bang from the little mower and a rebel yell from Mick. What a job, viewing the achievement made it all worthwhile, though the toll on Mick's back and the cider supplies to keep him going were significant.

The weather turned in sympathy with Mick's back pain giving him a well-earned rest indoors and time for us to catch up on paperwork and more research on all things to do with smallholdings. Looking through the ads Mick spotted an old David Brown tractor for sale locally at a really good price and was chuffed to find it was still for sale. After his recent experiences with land maintenance and following Ab's advice he realised the right tools for the job were rather bigger than our small hand mower and so a tractor was needed, closely followed by the right attachments to keep the ground in good order. Mick had also recently become the proud owner of the chassis and wheels for a 3 ton tipping trailer rescued from the far corner of a farmer's field, which when rebuilt and towed by a tractor would be great for large scale loads and spare his back. The tractor was duly bought and brought home, although looking very tired, being vintage, I could see Mick having hours of fun restoring it to former glory, especially as he had recently become a bona fide member of the David Brown owners club.

The toy store was now complete, JCB, Tractor, Quad and two trailers. Now if the weather ever stayed fine long enough we were ready for the really big jobs.

Animal outbuildings

Not having a yard with animal outbuildings was a serious disadvantage if we were to be serious about keeping sheep and pigs. We needed to have buildings for winter housing, medical attention and recovery close to the paddock. The ideal being to create a permanent building which would serve a multitude of purposes and have easy access from all areas.

The centre point of our proposed 'yard' was to be a full height permanent block building divided into bays to be used for farrowing (giving birth) and enable piglets and sow to be separated when needed, and also be used for sheep and lambs at other times. To give access to both sheep and pigs the building would be located in the corner closest to the upper garden by the old oak giving access to the paddock from the rear and to a new enclosure at the front which was intended as an outdoor pen for the pigs which would lead to another dual purpose run with a shelter in it for 'overflow' use by sow and piglets once they had been weaned or by ewes and lambs as a nursery. At last Mick was happy with the layout and location; close to the boundary with the garden but well out of reach of any old trees. The resulting buildings would be well drained and sheltered by the hedge as well as easily accessed with potential for adding more enclosures, as they were needed.

After much measuring and calculation a long list of the materials needed for the base and building of the main housing were given to our local builders merchant in Llandovery. Two days later they delivered everything as close to the cottage as the lorry could get which was in the parking area opposite the cottage. When they had finished it looked like a building site, piles of timber, stacks of concrete blocks, sacks of cement and huge bags of sand, all needing to be transported round to the paddock site. The fleet of boy's toys came into their own; JCB lifting sand bags onto the trailer, which was then hitched to tractor for the first of many trips down the lane and round to the paddock. The blocks were the biggest challenge, so heavy that only one could be picked up at a time. It was a great workout; a lot cheaper than gym membership and guaranteed us both a great nights sleep.

Sue, one of the wardens at St Barnabas and our closest neighbour, living off the main lane up the hill introduced Mick to her hubby Pete and son Les, experienced self builders who were happy to help with advice and even offering to help with laying any concrete bases. The latter would need to be done as one operation before the concrete went off and depending on the size might be beyond just Mick and I so reassured and with a rare dry couple of days forecast Mick began digging out the turf and setting the timber formwork in place to hold the cement base for the main outbuilding.

A week later and racing to finish before the weather broke Mick worked hard; ferrying loads of sand and cement bags using the quad and trailer then making sure the base was level before prepping with sand screed and a damp proof membrane. I did my bit by running an electric line from the house, got a bin full of water ready in place with hose ready to refill and laid out all the shovels and rakes we had. Pete and Les arrived with another wheelbarrow, rakes, and most importantly, cement mixer. The sun shone as they set to, one mixing and the other two spreading and levelling with the rakes before tamping the mix down firmly with a length of timber across the full width; keen to crack on before the weather broke, which in the valley was pretty much a certainty at sometime during the day.

Sue arrived at midday to see how it was going just as it started to drizzle. The lads doubled their efforts whilst we watched with a mug of tea from a comfy dry seat in the old caravan in the garden. Whilst getting to know each other we realised we had a lot in common, one shared love being home wine making. I dug out my well used wine bible by 'Mrs Gennery Taylor' which had recipes from A-Z for country wines and we spent a happy hour swapping recipes and planning how to increase our varieties and stock to best effect, identifying where to find all the free fruit flowers and berries we would need throughout the year. Carried away by with thoughts of unlimited supplies of free fine wine for us and provision as gifts for friends and family we suddenly realised the last mix of concrete was being poured and quickly decamped to the paddock gate to cheer the lads on as the base was finally completed.

Apart from building work another thing they all had in common was a liking for cider, making it easy to reward them for all the hard work. It was the beginning of a good friendship. Base completed we looked forward to starting on the walls as soon as the concrete had fully set, the weather thought otherwise and a day later the heavens opened again.

Big Pig

Taking another weather forced but well earned rest we took the opportunity to wander up to the Royal Oak. A chance bar stool chat with one of the locals gave Mick potential good news on the pig front, a man in the next valley was going to sell off his pigs, two of which were sows supposedly in pig. We talked it through and agreed it would be a great way of developing our experience from start as it were to finish when the piglets became porkers and went on to provide us with pork until the next litter. Also, yet to know how we would cope with the whole slaughter process it would be comforting to know that the mum would be staying with us for the foreseeable future. Decision made our resident bar stool pal, Duncan, offered to check with the pig man when we could go over and get his contact details for us.

It would be a while before the permanent outbuilding would be completed, and as it was only intended for winter pig housing we needed to get a pig ark in place on the 'summer run' ready for the sow's imminent arrival. Back at the builder's merchants, Mick sourced everything he needed within two days and had the ark built within three. He also made a timber platform for it to sit on to cut down on drafts and stop any damp getting through. Building the ark next to the workshop on the driveway was really practical for tools and electric but getting it around the cottage, up to the veg garden and through to the pigpen would be something else. Luckily my brother was staying for the weekend and between the three of us we manhandled the heavy timber base round to the run with many breaks to recover the feeling in our arms. After recovering we went back for the three pieces of corrugated iron that formed the ark with a wooden back panel. It was a doddle to lift in comparison with the base. The main difficulty was trying to stop laughing as we carried it unsteadily overhead; like a drunken tortoise we finally swayed into the paddock and dropped the ark in place. Secured to the base we surveyed our nice new pig house, now all we needed was the pig!

As promised Duncan told us the pig man was ready to sell and after a quick call for directions we were on our way across to the guy's smallholding across the valley to Pumpsaint. We had set off bright and early, as the guy was keen for us to get there by 10a.m, when he fed the pigs so we could see them at their best. Not wanting to get lost we went the main route along the A40 to the Lampeter turn off along which Pumsaint was situated. We stopped at a feed store to ask directions and noticed a postcard in the window advertising 'weaners' for £30 each from the guy we were trying to find. The place was not far from the Dolagauthi Gold Mine so as we followed the narrowing single-track roads deeper into the countryside the brown mine signs and mine lifting machinery on the skyline kept us in the right direction. A short way past and we guessed we had reached the right place when alongside the road we saw a stone sty and very muddied paddock, albeit devoid of any sign of pig life.

In front was a very expensive looking house with equally expensive cars in the driveway, not quite the farmyard we were expecting. To the rear was a sprawling arrangement of giant cages housing exotic birds of all shapes and sizes with a beautifully landscaped garden. A guy in cut off denims came out and introduced himself as the owner, he had given up city life for alternative living and obviously had the means to do it, dabbling in anything that caught his fancy, hence the bird varieties from emus to cockatiels.

The pigs, he told us, were a reluctant disposal, they had to go because his neighbour ran a riding school, regularly bringing novices out on hacks along the quiet lanes, when out of the blue they were confronted by playing pigs squealing blue murder it caused mayhem, the spooked horses bolting, chaos followed by attempts to calm and reassure both horses and riders. Not wishing to cause further disputes, or a lawsuit, and in the absence of sufficient land to relocate the pigs selling was the only answer. He was pleased and reassured to know like him we wanted animals for the joy of keeping them rather than a commercial operation.

Filling a bucket with pignuts he rattled them as he advanced on the empty run yelling ' Pig, pig, pig' (what else!) to be met with a chorus of high pitched squealing and grunting as emerging from various parts of the undergrowth at the bottom of the run charged a mass of weaners of varying sizes. The weaners were wonderfully coloured in shades of gold, orange and copper, some with black spots and patches, some with white socks and patches.

They were fast but not as fast as the two sows that emerged behind them. The first was a tan colour with traditional long snout; she was big but nowhere as big as the following sow. This one had her eyes fixed firmly on the food bucket and with a speed totally belying her size and bowling over piglets in her path she was first to arrive and happily dive into the feed. She was gorgeous, a dark grey haired mammoth with gold hairs running through the grey and black spots along her sides. Her ears were more Dumbo than pig, pointing alternately skyward like radar dishes or lowered to demurely cover her eyes. It was her snout though which really endeared her; it was pushed as far back into her face as it could go giving her a wonderfully comic appearance. I was in love, all practical thoughts went out the window and I wanted her – luckily so did Mick.

We were told she had been running with the boar for the last three weeks and their performance very much suggested she would be producing a litter sometime in July. Apparently sows were pregnant for three months, three weeks and three days, nice and easy to remember. She had had 12 in her last litter, only two less than the number of teats she had! While telling us what a good mum she was a weaner flew through the air past us squealing with outrage at being tossed away from the feed bucket by the so called good mums snout. The caveat, 'as long as nothing is between her and the feed bucket' was added a bit belatedly.

Worried as to what midwifery skills would be involved Mick was reassured to hear that the pig just got on with it, all that was needed was a clean and dry shelter with plenty of straw with which the sow would build her nest and then produce the litter unaided, our only role would be to try and ensure the new born piglets didn't get rolled on when mum lied down, until the piglets were clued up enough to dodge her mass. Big Pig, as we automatically thought of her, was such an old hand at it that when her last litter was due she ignored the pig sty and was found in a far corner of the field in her own nest built from hedgerow and straw surrounded by her offspring all suckling contentedly, just what we novices needed to hear.

The weaners advertised at £30 each were from other sows and were 8 weeks old. As sows have between 6 and twelve piglets it was quite reassuring to know that even with keeping 1or 2 for us the money made from selling weaners would cover some of the costs of keeping them. If kept until they reached suckling pig weight at six months they would fetch around £70 each or the butchered meat e.g. chops, joints and sausages could be sold from the freezer. This all had to be weighed against cost of the sow, visits by the boar, feed and butchering costs and the commitment to being there to look after them. Whilst Big Pig could have 2 litters a year we wanted her and the piglets to have a good life and were hoping to only have one litter a year, which would make us self sufficient for pork products. As Big Pig got older we intended to keep one or two of litter to bring on as the new 'mums' and let Big Pig have a graceful retirement until she went to the big sty in the sky via the butchers leaving us with a final gift of a very large supply of sausages! Whether we could face that when the time came remained to be seen.

A deal was struck and we were to pick Big Pig up the next morning so she could be split off from the others and ensure she was hungry enough to follow food straight into the van. Armed with lots of notes on all things pig together with a list of food and basic medicinal remedies we felt more confident that we could make this work. We stopped at the feed merchants on the way out to stock up on pignuts and maize, the first items on our list.

On reaching home we tried to work out exactly how we would get her home in the van. The back double doors would be ok for loading her in, either side the van had built in cabinets, which would ensure she couldn't turn and do a runner. The side door would give her a way out when we got home. Only problem to be overcome was that the van was quite high off the ground and a substantial ramp would be needed for her to walk up. Mick spent the rest of the day converting an old door into a pig friendly ramp complete with non-slip surface courtesy of the best bit of our old kitchen rug held in place with wood runners, the final result definitely pig friendly. The demise of the rug a welcome price to pay, plus the added bonus of less hoovering!

Arriving back at Pumpsaint the next morning Mick reversed the back of the van as close as he could to the pigsty. The farmer living opposite came to watch the entertainment so we roped him into helping and also bought two bales of straw from him, which in due course would be pig bedding, but more importantly were needed now to shut off any escape route Big Pig might look for either side of the doors. The farmer and myself took up position behind each bale, Mick manned the doors and pig owner threw food through the side door to entice Big Pig up the ramp. All was prepared and the pigsty doors opened, Big Pig was definitely hungry and as per the plan started to make her way up the ramp, and then she decided it was unfamiliar ground and quickly reversed. This went on for about five minutes before hunger got the better of her and she got so far as having three trotters inside the van. A gentle push and then all three guys threw their weight behind the van door, with a resounding bang the deed was done and we had Big Pig safely in the van. We didn't realise it then but that was the easy part.

We decided to go the 'shorter' rural route home to avoid traffic, this winded up and down across the valleys and whilst giving the most fantastic views was offset by the sheer drops, blind bends and renowned lack of passing places. All this with the largest, heaviest moving load we had ever had. Big Pig was quickly finishing the food left on the floor of the van and I started to get worried about getting her home before she got stressed. Mick was concentrating on the road trying to balance the van and anticipate passing places as farmers started to begin their field rounds. I was hanging over the back of my seat talking to Big Pig and trying to keep her at the front end of the van as the remaining pig nuts rolled towards the back, despite best intentions she was reversing up and suddenly one of the back doors opened. I shouted, Mick tried to brake and keep on the road as I climbed over my seat to prevent her falling out. I reached the doors just as a trotter started to hit fresh air. Mick made it to the back door just as my arms were giving out trying to hold her rear end in and between us managed to manhandle the doors shut without any loss of any part of Big Pig. Mick tied up the doors as an added precaution and we set off again, only to have a repeat of the same problem half a mile down the road. This time we realised the cause was that when Big Pig backed up her enormous bum, the same height as the door lock, was rubbing it open. For the rest of the journey I rode in the back lying on top of one of the side cupboards with my hands between the back door lock and Big Pigs backside, which believe me from the angle I was lying at was immense. I thought I was in danger of losing one or both arms every time she moved backwards. We were only 5 miles from home but it seemed like 500 with all the slopes and climbs.

When we finally pulled into our pot holed lane I felt quite dazed, not sure whether with relief or from the lack of feeling in my arms. Mick drove the van straight down to the rear paddock gate, bumping across the field to the field gate at the back of the pigpen.

In my painful position just as I thought it couldn't get any worse Big Pig decided it was toilet time and incapable of moving I was trapped and closer to the rear end and rapidly ejecting substantial contents of a pig's bum than I ever hoped to be again! Mick manoeuvred the van so the side door was level with the gate to the pen and I was trying so hard not to breathe that I was becoming light-headed. Luckily as soon as Mick opened the side door Big Pig jumped straight out and none the worse for the journey, happily trotted around exploring her new home. I wished I was in such good form, arms covered in pig poo and devoid of feeling from the waist up it took me a lot longer to get out of the van, gasping for fresh air and manically waving legs and arms about to get the feeling back so I could get washed up and smelling of something sweeter.

While I went for a quick shower Mick took Tia to be introduced to Big Pig. This involved Tia running up and down the pen alongside Big Pig and bringing her sticks to play with. When she didn't respond Tia resorted to getting as close to her ear as she could and barking at her. Big Pig just ignored her and it was clear we would have no problems between them other than Tia being jealous if Big Pig got too much attention. This was simply resolved by letting Tia have a handful of pig pellets as compensation.

We had to do a quick turnaround to go and collect the ramp and straw bales, which we had had to leave, as there was no room for anything in the van other than Big Pig on the first trip. We left her contentedly munching a belated breakfast and set off. The journey to and fro was a lot less fraught, comfortable and easier on the nose than the previous one. Back with the straw we put a couple of bundles in the ark and Big Pig set to shaking it up and building her new nest.

Chicken picking

Now Big Pig was in residence I was becoming a chicken nag, the run was ready and I was keen to realise my dream of collecting freshly laid eggs for breakfast. That Saturday Mick took me to a poultry auction in the nearby village of Ffairfach. The auction sheds were packed with a huge variety of cages, from bantams to turkeys and even a pair of peacocks. In-between the rows a mass of bodies jostled along the cages, a packed mix of buyers, sellers, tourists and families on a day out. The noise from both birds and bodies was deafening. The lots numbered up to 650 and the sale had reached number 6. We joined the mass being slowly swept along the rows and tried to glean any information about the caged birds, but other than the breed and source the tags lacked anything to assist novices like us. The auctioneers walked along the tops of the cages rattling through the lots and bidding with such speed that within minutes we had lost the plot and didn't have a clue what was happening. It was entertaining to listen to, the singsong chanting of the auctioneer interspersed with good humoured banter from the bidders but we quickly realised we would not be getting any birds today. We collected a few breeder's addresses and agreed to put off purchase until we could see the birds out of the cages and get advice on exactly what would best suit our location and needs, away from the manic activity of the auction sheds.

Escaping the livestock sheds to the relative quiet of the outdoor sales and armed with burgers and mugs of tea we spent a couple of hours wandering round the other auctions on site, everything from tractors to army surplus. We quite liked the look of some old stone troughs that we thought would be ideal for pigs as they would resist any amount of attempted overturning by them intent on making wallows with the water. There is nothing more frustrating than having filled a trough having it promptly upended and emptied by a snout intent on a quick shower followed by a muddy bath! We hadn't reckoned on the popularity of anything 'rustic' for garden ornaments and our early enthusiasm quickly slumped as the bidding rose to daft prices. We lost all interest as the bids went over £100 and resigned ourselves to making do with our plastic imitations for a while longer.

The next day we went through our Smallholders mag and found a poultry breeder who was located just outside Brecon and arranged to visit that afternoon. After stopping at the Farmers Co-op to pick up a sack of layers pellets feed and bale of wood shavings for the shed floor we had a lovely run through the Beacons to the farm which was a picture postcard farm setting of farmhouse and outbuildings in stone and slate with a horse and foal watching our arrival over the field wall and a variety of chickens coming to greet us as we got out of the van. At the back of the yard was a large hi bay barn from which a young man appeared to show us round the stock who were divided by breeds in large pens, each compiling 50 or so birds. I didn't realise how many different types of chickens there were, from the typical cartoon farmyard hen to weird feathered puffballs from which it was impossible to tell, which end was which.

We learnt more practical information about chickens in the next half hour than we had found out ourselves in the last six months. By buying birds at 'point of lay' we would be guaranteed eggs within four weeks from all of them until they went into 'moult', an annual shedding of plumage during which they wouldn't lay, egg laying would be resumed once they came out of this state. He explained that moult was not a precise science and may or may not happen in the first year. Also, chickens only have a number of eggs, which can be laid, different breeds lay different average amounts in a year and some are more suited to hardy living than others. I had the idea that once their laying days were over they would end up as Sunday roast but apparently laying chickens put all their effort into laying the eggs and consequently stay scrawny, hardly the plump bird fit for roasting, so they at least would stay with us until their turned their toes up naturally. We wanted to be self sufficient in eggs and have some left over to sell to neighbours to help with the costs of looking after them, also as it was so wet in Rhandirmwyn we wanted breeds common to the area rather than anything fancy.

Following advice we opted for Black Rock, and Warrens, both were hardy and were suggested as ideal for our needs, being hardy and prolific egg layers, six would more than suit our egg requirements. The Black Rock as their name suggested was black with gold heads and necks and apparently very good layers, up to 250 a year. The Warrens were mainly brown but with different white markings mixed in and equally good layers. We decided on three of each and were asked to choose the ones we wanted. Faced with a constantly moving flock of some 50 or so chickens we just asked him to pick ones which looked good to him and had some distinguishing features so we could tell them apart. Armed with a large butterfly net and two cardboard boxes within minutes he had them netted, boxed and handed over to us. Three in each box they crouched down and didn't move all the way home. The Black Rocks were £6 each and the Warren £4.50, for the grand sum of £48.50 we should have an unlimited egg supply for the next three years.

On returning home we left the chucks in the boxes while we added the finishing touches to their new home, laying shavings, hanging a pellet feeder a foot from the floor and putting in the water dispenser raised on a block to minimise spillage, all completed we were ready to let the girls see their new home. To settle them in we had been told to leave them in for a couple of days and that they should begin to lay in the next couple of weeks. Gingerly opening the tops of the boxes, we expected them to be fighting to get out, no, they were quite happy where they were so we closed the door and spied on them through the side window.

A head suddenly poked up out of each box, obviously the look outs for the group, swivelling round in all directions before disappearing back into the box to report to the troops that the coast was clear, within seconds all six had abandoned the boxes, exploring the new home followed by a fight to establish the pecking order on the ladder roosts, losers getting the lower rungs. Safely settled in we turned our attention to getting nesting boxes in place. Whilst in the local garden centre I found two plastic cat boxes in the sale, which minus the front doors would make excellent nesting for the chucks, fully enclosed but ventilated, they would be easy to clean, private and cosy for maximum egg production. An added bonus was that with the doors back on they could be used to keep sick ones in or transported as needed. Duly positioned on the two tree stumps we began checking them three times a day for our first eggs.

Next day we left the door open for them to explore the run. They came out in a stream, wings flapping and legs pumping as they ran along enjoying the freedom and fresh air. Within minutes they were happily scratching and pecking at the overturned branches we had set in place to reveal tasty snacks below. Getting them back in the shed at night was a breeze; as soon as dusk fell they had an inbuilt instinct to head in and get as high up as possible to avoid anything that might fancy a chicken takeaway. To stop them escaping the run we had been advised to clip their wings so they wouldn't be able to flap over the fence. We wanted them to be totally free range so didn't bother and they quickly got used to jumping onto the top of the fence and then flapping over into the paddock or garden where they happily spent the day wandering and we wasted lots of time watching their antics, before they headed back to the run at dusk. This was fine when days were short but as the days lengthened it would become a game of hunt the chicken as they started to wander further afield. Chickens may be rightly titled bird brained but they are not daft in working out where the food was coming from and so we got them used to following the rattling jug of layer pellets being taken from the caravan where all feed was stored across to the chicken shed.

Tia's bone hiding dug out under the caravan had been requisitioned by the chucks for dust bathing and if not in the run they could normally be found under there at the end of the day. Jug rattling they would run dementedly behind us and bounce up and down at the run fence, having decided that just because they found their own way out, we should help them back in. If we hovered over them they squatted down, flattening themselves to the ground making it easy for them to be lifted over the fence. If they thought it was too early to go to bed they made off up and down the fence with us diving after them, no fun when it was tipping down with rain! Tia then took it on herself to act as backstop, making sure they didn't reverse she herded them back to us. This became the accepted routine, the chucks seemed to like the contact and being carried home. The proof was in the nest boxes the next day, our first three eggs! We celebrated with a breakfast of freshly poached eggs on toast; the enormous yolks of deep bright yellow with firm whites were so tasty we decided we had bought our last from a supermarket! After a fortnight we were getting six a day and our first small step to self-sufficiency had been achieved.

Pride goes before a fall

At long last we seemed guaranteed a spell of dry weather and so decided to get another essential outside job done, overhauling the old woodshed in the front garden so it could be properly stocked with logs for the winter. At the moment it looked more like it should be used on a fire than stocking the wood for them. We were surprised it hadn't blown down by now, it was only held up by the hedge and brambles, missing timbers and holes in the iron roof not keeping anything dry inside. Renovation was not an option desperate measures were needed. Using the quad with a rope round one corner post, gently pulling away the shed gracefully collapsed in on itself. All the rotten stuff was loaded on the trailer to add to the woodpile, the roof with careful repositioning and sealing would be salvageable and so was stacked to be reused later. Because of the slope of the garden to the lane Mick used the JCB to bring the level up and make a nice solid base with scalpings before rebuilding the shed walls of shiplap timber. My job was to creosote all the timber, really cleared the sinuses! The back and sidewalls joined to the new frame, the roof was then replaced and bolted down, albeit due to rotten bits rather haphazardly but hopefully watertight. That evening looking out of the kitchen window it made a pleasant change to see an attractive solid looking woodshed rather than the collapsing pile which had been there in the morning. Reassuring thought that if it was raining Mick would be in the dry for wood chopping and log basket filling.

The next day was bright and sunny so the push was on to finish off and get the wood back in. A final covering of scalpings was all that was needed to finish the job. Mick fetched a scalpings load behind the quad and started to reverse the trailer whilst I was keeping Tia out of the way, checking the log pile, which would shortly be in its new home. Then came an almighty crack, followed by manic revving of engine as the fully loaded trailer crashed into the supporting centre post, cracking it right through before coming to a halt halfway in the shed. Because of the weight on it the quad couldn't pull the trailer out, mud flew from the wheels in all directions. Tia and I hid the other side of the hedge whilst Mick told the trailer exactly what he thought of it, I just hoped anyone walking along the lane didn't think he was ranting at me.

When the volume subsided we slinked round to offer moral support, Tia bearing a large branch to start off the wood pile and me with a shovel to help offload the scalpings so the trailer would be light enough to drag out, tactfully ignoring the deep ruts in the lawn caused by the futile wheel spinning of the quad. Hey ho, centre support replaced and scalpings tamped down the new log shed was finally ready for use and we were ready for a well-earned drink. We carried a bottle and some crisps up to the top of the paddock and sprawled on the slope looking round the valley had an impromptu picnic to celebrate. Sun still shining, Tia happily curled up next to us, what a lovely end to the day. Lesson learned, fully loaded trailer to be pulled by something more powerful than the load!

Piggy pregnancy, piglets, piglets and yet more piglets!

Big Pig was fed twice a day and in her pregnant state as much as she wanted. We quickly realised that the suggestion that pigs cost virtually nothing to feed because they ate all our left overs was a big porky (pardon the pun!). With only two of us there were precious little left overs of any substance, hardly a treat for the chickens, let alone a large pregnant pig. This changed though as word got out that we had a good home for all unwanted fruit and veg waste. Not sure if it was due to recycling interests or the anticipation of sharing in future pork products but bags started appearing with regularity, either at the top of the lane dropped off en route to church which we collected during our walks with Tia or dropped over our gate by walkers. Enthusiastic veg growers were also glad to know they would have a home for much larger amounts when they cleared their plots of the unwanted end of season crops.

Big Pig had an open buffet treat at least twice a week, from onions and tomatoes to banana and melon skins, she worked her way from one end to the other only lifting her head when the last scrap had disappeared, when, with a big smile on her face she pushed her head up for a scratch behind the ears before going for a nap, happy pig! We still needed to get in substantial feed supplies for her regular feeds, pig nuts, barley maize and corn sacks became a regular order from the Farmers Co-op in Llandovery. In the absence of a purpose built feed store the old caravan had inherited the job, with the added advantage off the ground and so rat proof as well as being really close to the runs and water tap needed for mixing some of the feed, my kitchen jug having been requisitioned for measuring it out.

Food sources sorted we felt our animal husbandry skills were developing nicely. Big Pig was better than an alarm clock as far as food was concerned, charging out of her ark grunting with expectation of instant service, which if not forthcoming immediately sent her into a high pitched squealing session, trotting up and down the fence nearest to the caravan until food was produced. With her increasing bulk this activity quickly made a deep muddy trench, which added to the fun of trying to get the food bucket into her run and safely placed without her trapping us against the fence, bowling us over or spilling the bucket contents in the mud. Distracting her long enough for us to get in the run was the simple part, it then became like a rugby game trying to dodge pig to get to a firm and dry patch of earth to put the food bucket on and get ourselves out of the way as she thundered towards it, submerging her head in the bucket with grunts of joy and upending it when it was empty, the piggy equivalent to us closing our knife and fork.

As Big Pig grew in size she wanted more attention, scratching behind the ears progressed to rubbing her butt and tickling her tummy, just as you would for any expectant mother. After prolonged tummy tickling one afternoon her eyes slowly closed and she keeled over, all four trotters outstretched, I thought I'd killed her! Kneeling down and gently stroking her I quickly realised that she simply wanted a massage! I rubbed and scratched all the mud away from her tummy, around her snout and even from her eyelids as with eyes closed and a smile on her face she dozed contentedly emitting gentle grunts of happiness. As we got to the end of June Big Pigs belly left us in no doubt that she was definitely pregnant and during one of the now regular massage sessions I was overwhelmed to feel movement in her belly from numerous little kicks and ran to get Mick to feel for himself. What a moment, how could I explain to my city colleagues the feeling of complete happiness and contentment to be got from sitting in a field caressing a pregnant pig!

Our rural life 'bible', Home Farm by Paul Heiney, informed that fresh grazing greatly assisted a sow's vitamin and mineral intake for both her and the piglets benefit. As the paddock grass was springing into life again after Micks marathon cut it was an ideal time to leave the gate to the pig pen open letting Big Pig decide if she wanted to venture out and forage, did she! She sprinted out, making straight for the lush grass around the tree cages and chomped away with gusto, stopping to raise her head up to sniff out new tasty treats, a comic picture with clumps of grass out of each side of her mouth. Her pregnant state didn't affect her wanderlust to roam around the paddock, especially up to the top of the bank where the old oaks had shed layers of acorns, which are the piggy equivalent to a tray of your favourite chocolates. Any concern that she wouldn't want to come back to the ark in the evenings were quickly dispelled, the minute the food bucket was rattled she charged down the slope at speed, belly swinging from side to side, us watching in concern, worried in case she rolled over, or even failed to stop at the fence, but with the food bucket as her goal she went from lightening speed to dead halt as soon as her snout hit the grub. Routine established we awaited the next sign of imminent litter arrival, which would be signs of nest building and milk coming into her teats.

At the end of the first week in July I noticed grass was being collected into the corner of the ark atop the straw we had provided, a good sign that Big Pig intended to give birth there and not out in the paddock. Giving her regular massage gave the opportunity to check her teats for milk, gently squeezing, no sign yet, though the increasing kicking and wriggling in her tummy let us know things were well on the way. Not to be caught out Mick made a wooden frame about a foot high and wide which slotted along one side of the ark would give an escape area for the piglets to sleep in safety without mum rolling on them, I wondered how they were supposed to know how to use it?

As Tia and I returned from our early morning walk each day Big Pig would normally be pacing the pound ready for her breakfast but today there was no sign. As I peered round the corner of the ark I was taken aback to see her laid full stretch suckling nine piglets! No gory bits, no signs of distress, just a perfect picture of mother grinning from ear to ear gently grunting encouragement to the chorus of sucking mouths clamped firmly to their bespoke teat. I watched in awe of what for me was a magical moment, to see the joy of Big Pig and the new beginning of life for our first herd was overwhelming, tears of happiness and relief rolled down my face as I retreated quietly (quite unlike me!!) until I was safely out of the pen, and then burst in babbling incoherently to Mick who used to my ravings was out to the ark before I'd drawn breath. We proudly watched them suckle, all were looking content, tiny little golden bundles, down to the Tamworth boar, some with black patches, some with white socks, each adorable. Big Pig raised her head and grunted to us as if to say, "what's all the fuss? I'm the expert here!" and in complete agreement we left her in peace to bond with the new arrivals.

After a celebratory breakfast of poached eggs freshly collected we went back out to check all was well and feed Big Pig. She was stood outside the ark grunting at Mick to get a move on. While she tucked in I checked inside and was amazed to see the nine piglets all curled up in a heap together under the creep frame as intended. Checking the birth bedding I threw out the wet straw and found another piglet, still in its birth sack, it had obviously been born dead and put to one side by Big Pig. Mick took it away while I laid a fresh straw bed. Whilst cooing over the litter Big Pig came back in and they all scrambled around the straw to get to her as she started to drop her enormous bulk on one side to feed them. It was an anxious moment and we did interfere trying to pull the little ones out of the way, seeing for ourselves how easy it would be for one to be inadvertently crushed. Once down the piglets made a beeline for their teat, clambering over mum and each other, without fail they always latched onto the same one. All teats looked the same, no numbers or names above to help out, just an instinctive pull to the first one they had taken from. I felt sorry for the ones who had drawn the teats on the right side as that was Big Pigs favourite side to lie on and if she flopped too far their teats were trapped under her tummy. Squealing madly and legs a pumping they dived under her belly to latch on while the 'lefties' climbed on top of them to reach their free-swinging teats above. One or two went for the wrong teat and were knocked off by the rightful owner, causing them to frantically scramble over or wriggle under their siblings to find the right one. The pitch of the squeals really put your teeth on edge; imagine hundreds of saucepans being scraped with metal spoons at the same time. Just as it reached fever pitch all mouths found milk and there was instant silence from the piglets and a contented grunting from Big Pig, bliss. This was to be repeated four to five times a day for the first week or so with the piglets then crawling into their bedding and sleeping soundly until it was feeding time again, Big Pig only leaving the ark when we fed her or to do her business, well away from her nest.

Mick had decided we would spare the piglets, and us, the farmers recommended 'teeth and tackle' removal. Its purpose was to a) prevent damage to the mother's teats or injury to each other and b) ensure no inbreeding or testosterone causing bad behaviour and bad meat. This was unnecessary as far as we were concerned as we only intended Big Pig to have one litter a year and to wean the piglets at 8 weeks before the teeth became a problem, equally the free range life they would have would give them no reason for frustration and aggression so common in the confines of intense breeding conditions. As for the other end, we would not be keeping any boars and they would be gone before they reached sexual maturity so we wanted them to be able to enjoy their short lives as intact as nature intended. Besides for us novices it was a far easier way to tell them apart from the gilts, their tummies were not always visible but their rear ends were and we were able to see we had the ideal balance of five boars and four gilts. Despite concerns of crushing and my over reacting by trying to be there whenever Big Pig laid down no losses occurred in the first two weeks and I began to relax.

All nine piglets had different colours and markings, from totally ginger to a mix of predominantly bright ginger with a wide variety of black spots and patches, white legs and ruffs. They all had wonderfully bright eyes and the most endearing looks on their faces, think Babe times 9. Jumping all over mum and having races round the ark whenever she vacated, gradually venturing outside to play chase, darting in all directions, colliding and running off again. They started to boldly go further from mum, then wherever they were they would stop dead in their tracks for apparently no reason, as if playing statues, snouts quivering before squealing loudly and running back to Big Pig as fast as their little trotters would carry them.

Tia appointed herself nursemaid and guard. She would sit for hours alongside the fence, getting as close as possible she would lay alongside Big Pig watching the piglets, leaping to her feet and barking at them if they became too boisterous, gently whining when they were feeding. As they grew in size and confidence they ran up to her and she would lick them through the fence, gently nibbling their ears, I hoped in affection and not in anticipation of the much larger dry cured pigs ears we bought her as treats!

The favoured spot for the tribe was at the bottom of the run next to the chickens, who were quite undeterred by this invasion of what must have been the animal equivalent of football supporters invading the pitch having won the match. The chucks lined their side of the fence, heads jerking from side to side watching the game with intensity, trying to work out whether food was involved which they could also make a play for. They quickly became bored when there was no evidence of any grain at all and went back to attacking the remains of the cabbage roots in their run.

When Big Pig started reducing the piglets suckling times we started to feed them 'growers nuts', aptly titled for what they were and how they behaved. To start with organising separate feeding in the pen was not a problem as Big Pig was given her bucket outside the ark, then the piglets trough, which in theory all nine could line up and get a fair portion from, was filled at the top end of the pen next to the fence, giving the tribe enough time to eat their fill before mum charged over and tossed them out of the way in her eagerness to finish any food left. Best laid plans were quickly thwarted as the piglets got bigger, bedlam ensued as they beat us to the trough before we could get the food in and we were caught in a jumble of trotters and snouts trying to secure the biggest section of the trough, either by getting a couple of trotters in the way of their neighbours or quite ingeniously laying in the trough to hide the grub until they were ready to eat it. The latter was a daft idea as the rest simply pushed them along the trough with their snouts and carried on eating as the indignant piglet ended its ride along the trough by being unceremoniously dumped off the end. Still that was a better result than if Big Pig was on the food hunt as she simply upended the whole trough sending piglets and food flying everywhere. Another tack to ensuring being first for food was that they took to sleeping in the trough during the day, like New Year sale shoppers intent on being first in the queue at opening time.

To make sure the piglets got a fair share we started feeding Big Pig in the paddock where she stayed until the piglets had finished, this had the added advantage of her doing what comes naturally in the paddock and not in the pen, significantly reducing mucking out. Once finished she simply grazed until the gate was reopened and they swapped positions, checking out each other's troughs to see if there were any scraps left.

As they got bigger the piglets started to develop characters that suited their appearance. The lead characters resembling the Great Escape planning committee: completely ginger the thinker of the group, laying watching everything, madly spotted with black the scavenger, forcing the fence to steal the sheep's nuts or chickens bread if it fell close enough, white legs and ruff the boss, strutting round with the others deferring to him and black eye the cocky escape artist, sprinting for freedom having managed to launch herself over the fence from the trough the others had upended to form a gangplank!

Finally a long overdue dry spell dried out the paddock enough to let the pigs have the run of it during the day, hopefully grazing the grass down and digging up any offending patches of bracken and tough grass. The piglets were a bit intimidated by the wide open spaces to start with and trotted in file behind Big Pig as she led the way to her favourite spot which was at the farthest corner of the paddock at the top of the slope where the fence joined a running brook, which ensured the ground was always soft and had been taken over by bracken giving good rooting, cover and shade, a pig paradise. We tried to keep count of the tribe but once they entered the bracken only mums back was visible, the violent thrashing about of the bracken around her the only clue that she had company.

I thought pigs were supposed to be lazy and so would stay in one spot, snuffling and sleeping for the day, neatly leaving the rest of the paddock unscathed. That myth was quickly dispelled as the piglets' confidence grew and with mum they started making circuits of the paddock boundaries, steadily chomping grass as fast as possible until a smell underneath would cause their snouts to wrinkle in ecstasy and result in complete uprooting of a patch to get to whatever had taken their fancy beneath before moving onto the next patch. The continual circuits and excavations caused a muddy track around the paddock to quickly appear, widening every forty feet or so to a large wallow turfed up by Big Pig who loved laying in the mud to cool down whilst the tribe ran on, chasing each other manically while she dozed happily. Her rest was short lived though as suddenly the piglets realised that mum's horizontal state meant teats were on offer and with frantic squealing a race and fight ensued to get back to their allocated feeding station before mum got cross and shook them off and resumed her patrol of the borders.

Welsh weather quickly reverted to type and the constant rain together with the pigs attention was causing the grass to quickly recede and be replaced by mud so the daily excursions were put on hold and the troops restricted to barracks until the weather and the paddock improved.

No sign of Big Pig this morning, normally she would be grunting in anticipation at the fence but today she was nowhere in sight. I banged the food bowl and with much grunting and banging against the arc Big Pig appeared limping badly on her front right foot. It was painful to watch her trying to hobble on the muddy uneven surface of the run, made worse by the recent torrential rain. As she stood eating I felt all over her leg and couldn't find any sign of injury. She had been ok last night so the instant lameness was rather worrying; still it hadn't affected her appetite so I left her to enjoy her breakfast while I went to get mine.

The post bought good news; we were now officially a registered smallholding with a registered herd of pigs and flock of sheep, the latter applied for in anticipation of having had them by now, still it would save time later. An accompanying leaflet from Defra titled 'information for the new pig owner' gave many useful tips and hints but rather alarmingly information on diseases which stated sudden lameness as a symptom of foot and mouth. My mind went into overdrive and I had poor Big Pig incinerated together with her nine piglets before I'd reached the end of the article, despite Mick's logic that infection was impossible as the recent outbreak was confined to Surrey some 200 miles away together with the fact that Big Pig had been in no contact with anything other than our livestock and us. I started to trawl the Internet for more help whilst Mick being the level headed practical one went out to Big Pig and examined the offending trotter whilst she was laid suckling the tribe, unlike my check whilst she was stood ankle deep in mud Mick's examination revealed that she had split her hoof and a bit was hanging loose, obviously the cause of the problem and giving her pain as soon as any weight was put on it.

Big sigh of relief and mental note to listen to Mick rather than my overactive imagination was followed by a quick phone call to Chris our farmer pal in Oxford who told us all it needed was a good clean, trimming the hoof then spraying it with antiseptic. As our medicine chest had nothing stronger than tea tree oil and dainty nail scissors I drove to the vets and came back armed with a wonderful 'fixes anything' antiseptic spray cum antibiotic for all animal injuries and a sturdy pair of hoof trimmers, very similar to garden secateurs but much sharper. Armed with these a toilet roll and the tea tree oil we sneaked into the ark where Big Pig was dozing and stroking her tummy teased out her right trotter from under her to clean and trim the split hoof, finishing with an attractive coat of turquoise antiseptic spray which I also enjoyed as I held the offending hoof for Mick to spray. It was difficult to tell if we had resolved the problem but by the smile on Big Pig's face she was pleased with the attention and we left her in peace.

The next day she seemed much better and we let her and the tribe back into the paddock to graze as it was much firmer for her than her run and didn't seem to hurt her foot as much. By the end of the day she definitely seemed on the mend, a sigh of relief and another mental note to not over react in future (yeah right!)

Trees and telephone lines don't mix

The weather forecast was good for two days with a return to rain and gale force winds shortly after. As I had a week off Mick decided it was ideal timing to try and cut back decaying tree branches overhanging the lane, threatening both the phone lines which threaded through them and walkers beneath. Past experience helping to fell the large trees at the back of the cottage had shown Mick how important safety was, however, lacking the 'cherrypicker' platforms to reach the dizzy heights needed he improvised by tying an extended ladder on the roll bar at the back of the cab on the pick up truck to preventing it tipping over whilst he stood on the uppermost steps with the chainsaw extended on a pole above his head aimed at the offending branches, at least he was wearing a hard hat! My role was to drive the truck; positioning it where needed and pulling the cut branches out of the way as we moved along the lane.

I was scared stiff watching the branches cracking and swinging down towards Mick and the van, but credit where credit's due, Mick really had become skilled with pruning, knowing exactly where to cut to get the branches to fall safely. Whilst coming close none of the branches threatened him or the ladder, though the van cab was taking a bit of a battering. The system was working very well, Mick cut the outer branches first to reduce weight as he moved back to the main branch which by then was clear of the phone lines. I placed the van each time before jumping out and pulling away all the fallen branches, though some were so big I ended up tangled in the middle waiting for Mick to lift them off. A couple of outer branches caught the precariously placed telephone line threaded between them all, but it reassuringly bounced them off and returned to its correct position, it was lucky it was so old and had so much play in it.

Encouraged by the results Mick decided to tackle a really big branch, which looked clear of the line except for the last bit of foliage. Just to be sure it fell the right way Mick decided to rope it and have me pull it away from the phone line when it was cut through. Returning from the garage with a length of rope weighted by a chain he proceeded to throw a loop over the branches. Each time it fell short or long and landed trapped in other trees or the fence and took an age to get it out. Six throws and some choice language later the rope was successfully tied and Mick cut through the branch. I threw my whole 7 ½ stone behind the rope pulling it to the right and it did the opposite, lifting me off the ground and launching itself to the left, straight over the phone line, crashing to the floor pulling the line with it which with an ominous pinging from the telephone pole snapped and flailed about wildy before joining the tangled mess below.

Silence. We looked at the gap where the branch and the phone line used to be. Far from disappointment Mick's first reaction was relief that the line was out of the way and he could now cut down the other rather large branches that he had previously been avoiding. I coiled the now redundant phone line up and placed it neatly at the foot of the oak responsible for its demise to be dealt with later and we carried on our lumberjack activities. As soon as we had finished the big stuff I went to find a kind neighbour who still had a phone to report the fault. One of the very few times not having a mobile signal was a disadvantage. Luckily only our phone lines and the remote sewage station at the bottom of the line came off the lane line so I could face the neighbours with a clear conscience. At the end of our lane stood a holiday cottage, luckily occupied by the owners Gwen and Peter who were at home, and happy to help.

Trying to report the fault was an exercise in patience. All I wanted was to tell a person that the phone line had pulled out of the pole connection and simply needed to be reconnected. Instead I spent over ten minutes on the phone pushing button answers to an automated fault service which informed me it had to first check the line to tell me if our phone was working, as I had witnessed first hand the demise of the line which caused our phone to die and was trying to report this simple fact I found the automated process rather stupid. Equally to be told that an engineer would come to check the line and find the fault within the next two days before allocating another engineer to fix it even more frustrating, still you cannot argue with a machine so I pushed all the right buttons, thanked Gwen for use of the phone (mental note to present half a dozen new laid eggs as proper thanks tomorrow) and wandered back down the lane to tell Mick the good news, no calls or broadband for the next couple of days.

The nine piglets were now definitely entering porker stage, no longer the cute snuffling toddlers, more rampant disrespectful teenagers high on punk rock. They were now weaned and trebled in size, in between rough housing each other finding and eating anything they could was the main pastime, the paddock was in danger of losing any growth it had had, this despite the huge amounts of growers' nuts and leftovers they were devouring twice a day. We decided it was time to reduce numbers to avoid gang warfare and let us make best use of the land. We had to concentrate on the porkers we would be finishing for the freezer later in the year.

With perfect timing, Ab from the Coleg Farm came to see how we were coping with raising the pigs; he had raised a herd in the past and was interested in doing so again. By the end of the visit Mick had agreed that he could have five of ours, some to bring on as sows to start a herd and some destined for the college kitchens, Ab was to collect at the end of the week. This was an ideal solution, the short trip along the lane to the Coleg would minimise any trauma for the pigs and having spent time at the farm and seen where they would be living we had no worries about their destination or treatment, especially as some would be spending their whole lives there. An added bonus would be being able to stroll up and visit to see how they were doing and compare notes.

I must confess to being pleased that on the day of departure I was in London and so when I arrived home Big Pig and the four remaining porkers were all snuggled up in the ark and their siblings were doing likewise in the college farmyard. Apparently all had gone well, Ab with student support chose their five from the nine and simply lifted them out of the enclosure with much indignant squealing which swiftly subsided when they were put in the trailer with nut snacks. Big Pig had not appeared unduly stressed at their departure and I was pleased to see that Mick had made sure the gilt (girl) Big Pig (and I) liked the best was one of the ones that had stayed.

From old pond to piggy heaven

A surprise opportunity enabled us to buy the redundant pond area next to our cottage, adjoining the lane. Almost an acre of land comprising man made banks which in times gone was fed water from a sluice to fill the pond which in turn, via a pipe running under the lane, fed the Crusher waterwheel which drove the lead crushing machinery. Over sixty years since use, and following sluice and pipe collapse the pond was such in name only. Incapable of holding water its broken clay/dirt base was overgrown with brambles and small trees, the banks hosting large oaks, with the run off area an uneven mess of tangled undergrowth and fallen trees. No good for building, grazing or restoring to pond without major outlay but an excellent solution to our land management problem. The 'pond' would become spring/summer HQ for the pigs until it became waterlogged when they would come into the winter quarters in the paddock pound. So sparing the paddock and giving the sheep, when we eventually got them, relief from piggy persecution for best part of the year.

Now all attention was turned to securing the boundaries and clearing anything that may cause pigs harm, not an easy or cheap job as the lane fencing and hedging needed urgent attention and the field boundary with our neighbours needed stock proofing. The varying heights made things difficult, as did the different conditions underfoot. One minute I was striding purposefully across firm ground, the next trapped in sucking clay, which needed Mick to pull me out of, having just splashed his way out of a boggy patch further along. A fortnight later we viewed a job well done, still a wild ground but hopefully a secure and safe one. Enough old iron, wire and glass had been found to fill a couple of skips and that was just what was on the surface! We settled for make and mend on the fencing as in the Autumn/Winter we wanted to plant new hedging which may affect the placement, we also wanted to work out the best way to use the area for the pigs, and more importantly the funds to do it. Ideally the area would become the piggy equivalent to a holiday home. Finally, Mick put in new gates from the top garden giving direct access from the pigpen to the pond area and we were ready to let the pigs have daily access. Until we were happy the boundaries were really secure we didn't want to risk leaving them there overnight.

To get from the pound to the pond the pigs had to cross the

top part of the veg garden. We tried to minimise escape with a motley barrier created by the picnic bench, upturned wheelbarrow and a few planks of wood. Mick would be stationed at the pen gate and I would open the gate to the pond with Tia standing guard along the barrier as Mick opened the pen and food bucket in hand led them out. This worked well for the four piglets who all followed straight into the pond area, Big Pig at the back decided she fancied a stroll around the garden so Mick turned back, trying to get her attention by rattling the food bucket, cue for the piglets to do a quick about turn and beat me back through the still open pond gate which I had neglected to shut. Chaos ensued as Big Pig continued her inspection of the garden, much more interested in our small orchard than Mick's endearments, which were slowing changing to threats as he resorted to trying to push her in the right direction, fat chance! Four manically squealing, grunting porkers criss crossed the veg patch at speed in different directions closely pursued by Tia and myself criss crossing equally manically, squealing and barking. Just as things reached fever pitch Mick called a halt and 'politely' asked Tia and I to leave him to it. Noise abated, Mick let everything calm down and then worked with Big Pig rather than against her to get his way.

Big Pig only liked to go forward when nothing obstructed her way so Mick waited until she came to the bottom fence where there was nothing to interest her and then resumed his enticement with pig nuts, snout twitching she decided the bucket was a better option than the chicken run and followed him slowly back up the garden, into the pond area and a delayed breakfast. Under orders Tia and I stayed well back as the piglets appeared from their excavations in various corners of the veg garden to join mum. Mick shut and secured the gate with a look in my direction which sent me scuttling to let the chickens out and collect eggs for a conciliatory if much-delayed breakfast.

The pigs loved their daily outings into the old pond, pushing for pole position to get over there first, snuffling away at the layers of rotten leaves and acorns built up over the years as the oaks surrounding the pond bank shed both in large amounts. Coupled with the soft pond bottom it was piggy heaven. We rather hoped that with all their snuffling the cracked clay beneath the growth would be puddled together and in a year or two we would have a watertight base to create a smaller pond, which would let us expand to ducks and geese. Ironically they preferred to plough up the top of the banks where the acorns were most in evidence and only used the pond itself for racing each other to the next tasty bank spot. Still, they were really enjoying life and it was a joy to see them behaving naturally.

The porkers seemed to grow by the hour. The biggest gilt, the favourite, now known unsurprisingly as Little Pig, we had decided was to stay with us and become a breeding sow with her mum. Little Pig was a wonderful mix of colours, bright copper ears and body with black spots all finished with a white ruff and legs. She was the brightest of the bunch, quickly copying Big Pig in cornering her feed and making her nest. The other gilt was copper all over with the exception of three black streaks on her hindquarters; she was a free spirit, the first to find any weak fencing and force her way to freedom, regardless of what was on the other side. The biggest boar was totally copper coloured, he was a bit of a bully, always on the lookout for more food and continually waking up and rousing the others to a high pitched squealing chorus whenever he caught sight of us with anything resembling a food bag in hand. The other boar had similar marking to Little Pig with the exception of a big black patch over one eye earning him the name Bullseye, though I was told not to name the ones who would go as I would get too attached I couldn't help it as he was the smallest and after his escapist trick with the trough had endeared himself to me, I made sure he got his fair share of grub.

One morning Big Pig seemed really skittish, breaking into a trot at every opportunity and twirling round in circles whenever the others came close. Being novices we didn't know why at first but soon clicked on when the boys wouldn't stop sniffing round her rear end and whenever she stood still long enough tried to mount her. We couldn't stop laughing, as they were less than half her height and just slithered in a heap off the leg they launched themselves at. Yes, Big Pig was now in season and the boys at five and a half months had decided they wanted to prove themselves as boars. Now we had to deal with the problem of keeping them out of her way to avoid them being damaged by her increasingly annoyed rebuttals. That evening all five trotted back to the pens but were neatly split, the three who would be leaving us diverted into the original pig pen with the metal arc freshly piled with straw and Big and Little Pig continued on into the permanent pigpen without a backward glance.

This was timed nicely with the constant rainfall making the pond area too wet for man or beast. In the pigpen Big and Little Pig had the benefit of a good concrete base to walk around when the dirt compound became so muddy that they sunk up to their teats and were in danger of pulling a muscle trying to get out, the porker three were not so lucky. They quickly became indistinguishable from the mud they were ploughing through in their pen which was now resembling the Somme so Mick decided to ensure their remaining memories were happy ones and relocated them in the paddock using the covered trailer as a temporary home for them. Using the trailer served a dual purpose, the first would be they would be off the ground in the dry and the second was that they would become familiar with going in and out of the trailer, reducing stress when it was time to leave us.

Sheep at last!!

A chance conversation in church with our new warden Dawn resulted in introduction to her sister and brother in law, Margaret and Tony, who owned a sheep farm across the Towy valley and also looked after her father's flock. They kindly invited us up to find out exactly what we needed, and to advise us as to what we should get before hopefully buying them from them.

The journey to Tony and Margaret's was across the Towy bridge along the same windy country lane we had taken to collect Big Pig, though at least their farm was this side of the valley. It only took us twenty minutes to get to their drive, which was a steep climb up to the farmhouse. The views were spectacular. Margaret and a really cute puppy that was an unlikely mix of Collie and Jack Russell, the best of both farm breeds, greeted us. Tony appeared from the nearby sheds and we got to know each other over a welcome mug of tea seated round the Raeburn and eating the nicest freshly baked fruitcake I've ever tasted. They were really kind in explaining all the practicalities involved in having sheep and happy to ensure we not only started our flock properly but also would be available to mentor us as we developed in experience. We felt in safe hands and reassured that guided by them we could make a go of creating our own flock and be self sufficient in lamb as a result.

With the arrival of their son Ryan to help we went to walk their fields and see the different types of sheep they had to decide which would be best for us. Having described the extent and type of land we had they recommended either the black Welsh or speckle faced sheep, both local breeds well used to valley slopes, mountains and the ever present wet weather. Basically bomb proof for novices, exactly what we were looking for. We were originally thinking of having six lambs for fattening and then slaughter on an annual basis but Tony and Margaret suggested the best thing to do was to keep ewes which would be serviced by a ram in October/November to ensure lambs each Spring. This would ensure the paddock was maintained but not overused and also give us self-sufficiency in lamb without annual outlay on lamb purchase. We could see the practical sense in this and from a personal perspective as with the pigs I very much liked the idea of having resident mums who we could bond with offsetting the loss of the lambs each year. We were concerned though as to how we would source a ram at the right time, their solution was to either borrow or purchase one from them.

We quite liked the idea of black sheep as they were different from any of our immediate neighbours, they were slightly smaller than the speckle faced though and a practical issue raised by Margaret was that if you needed to mark them or recognise them easily their colouring made it quite difficult. The speckle faced varied in colouring from pure white with speckle black/white faces to patchy white and black with pure black faces and each one was easily identified, this for us would be a plus, as was the larger size which promised bigger lambs and more meat. We then looked at the rams, which were white and due to breeding would be used with the black ewes. By then we had decided we would like the speckle faced ewes so the white rams weren't an option and it looked like buying a ram would not be an option. We were a bit disappointed, as we had come round to the idea of not having to impose on them to borrow one and be self sufficient for breeding. Ryan then suggested looking at a ram they would not be using again which was marking time in with their Jacobs ewes, which were not for sale. The Jacobs looked more like mountain goats than sheep with their elegant horns and close fleeces, not for us, but strutting across with a definite swagger and air of disdain was a large black ram, love at first sight! More dark grey than black he was magnificent, big curled horns he oozed masculinity and arrogance, a real Rambo!

We wanted him to be the daddy of our flock!! It was agreed we would have four speckle face ewes and the ram. Tony and Ryan corralled the ewes and asked us to choose the ones we wanted and they would ID them with a coloured spray and bring them down to us at the weekend. Mick let me choose the first but I took so long and chose the cutest fluffiest white smallest one which probably wasn't the best way to select our future breeding stock so Mick took over guided by Ryan to make sure the remaining three were chosen by head rather than heart.

Deal done we had to decline a kind invite to stay for supper to get home and feed the pigs, though it would have been very easy to stay put in the warm kitchen chewing the fat with our new found friends, easygoing with a good sense of fun, happy to help us learn how to get the best from our holding and pleased we wanted to be involved in restoring and working the land. It was a nice feeling to have, a sense of belonging, a sense of place. The next morning Mick went down the valley to the Farmers Co-op to stock up on lamb nuts and buy a couple of long troughs to put in the paddock ready for the sheep's arrival. Tony had already loaded Mick's van with hay bales the day before so we were well stocked for winter food supplements until the grass started growing properly again in the Spring. At long last we were about to get our flock.

As promised Tony and Ryan arrived towing a small animal trailer containing the four ewes and black ram, running it down the lane and straight onto the paddock so averting any attempted escapes. The porkers were to be confined to barracks, in their trailer until the flock were in residence and they were sleeping contentedly after a big breakfast. Opening the rear door of the sheep trailer down it formed a ramp onto which the four ewes quickly jumped out and made off onto terra firma, stopping almost immediately in a group to nibble the grass. The complete contrast of approach to that exhibited by the pigs was amazing, the sheep delicately picking their way across the paddock, stepping gingerly or jumping over suspect patches to daintily nibble at the short grass shoots, ignoring anything else and delegating one lookout to alert the group to any threat which caused them to flock together and move as one until they felt safe again and they moved apart to repeat the cycle. In contrast pigs make a cavalry charge, chomping and rooting up anything in sight as though there is no tomorrow, oblivious to anything until its on top of them and they then all cry out in panic and run off. Our flock leader was yet to emerge from the trailer. Rambo had been separated from the girls for the journey to prevent any close quarter damage from his horns, or worse as the girls were in season, any premature attempt at copulation, which in such close confines, could have been catastrophic. Looking down his nose at us from behind his partition he managed to look both affronted and ready for revenge at the same time. Tony wisely opened the dividing gate from outside the trailer so he wasn't in the line of fire, with his confines removed we were expecting a charge for freedom but true to character Rambo flexed his muscles, shrugged his shoulders and looking menacingly first to the right, then the left, slowly swaggered out of the trailer and then with a look of anticipation on his face quickened his pace towards the girls curling his lip as arrived to show an evil grin with his head raised to the sky giving them a good view of his magnificent horns in profile. Tony told us this grinning and raising the head was part of the mating game and showed that the girls were in season and deserving of Rambo's attention. As it was now autumn when their flocks traditionally came in season if all went to plan we would be looking forward to lambing in the warmth of Spring. Not wishing to be voyeurs we left them to sort themselves out having found out from Tony that other than feeding with nuts once or twice a day and keeping the hay rack and water trough full we would not need to interfere with them until six weeks before lambing when all would need injections to protect them and their lambs from numerous infections, which they kindly offered to do for us so we would know how to do them in the future. For any other problems we had their home and mobile numbers and were urged to call if we needed anything.

Later that day we let the porkers out and were pleasantly surprised at how the two different groups got on, the sheep had no interest at all in the pigs and the pigs quickly lost interest trying to get them to react to their attention, a truce was declared and they worked round each other to good effect. There followed a period of calm, Big and Little Pig were happy, the flock were settled in, if Rambo's cheesy grin was anything to go by we would be doubling its size in the Spring and the three porkers were more than happy living the single life with no responsibilities.

Walking Tia along the hedgerows I was feeling disappointed that there was nothing to fill my ever-present carrier bag with bounty to turn into wine or jams, the only berries being well frosted sloes which I found really bitter. I suddenly remembered the large bottle of gin languishing at the back of the pantry; we didn't drink it but were loathe to just throw it out. Bought years ago for Granddad on his occasional visits when he would have one small G&T, it unfortunately had outlasted him. Knowing how he hated waste and how he loved the countryside I thought it would be fitting to make sloe gin in his honour. Hoping the results would be tastier than the raw berries I set to and managed to make a small demijohn full that I left at the back of the pantry for tasting in three months time, shaking regularly as recommended. I must confess after two months I forgot it was there until the following year when prompted by the new years harvest! Digging it out and gingerly unscrewing the top thinking I would putting it out of its misery down the toilet I was pleasantly surprised by the lovely autumnal smell and even more so by the taste. Gosh it was strong but the resulting warmth and well being the aftertaste left was really, really good. More by luck than design I had produced a really good sloe liqueur which drunk out of small sherry glasses would make an excellent aperitif or if out and about a welcome addition to the hip flask. I strained the liquid off the sloes and bottled in two small wine bottles, nicely labelled and decorated they would make lovely presents as long as I issued them with a warning to sip not gulp! I now make this every year.

Sloe Gin Recipe:
Prick with a fork ½ pint of sloes and place in bowl
Mix in ½ pint of gin and ½ pint of sugar, cover and leave for two days, mix again then bottle or put in jars together with the sloes.
      Shake weekly and taste after three months, if not to your taste leave it until it is (I would leave it until the following year) then strain and bottle.

The circle of life

Church was proving the contact point for all our needs, Mick a committed atheist found this rather unsettling. This week I met a lovely lady, Hazel and beautiful small daughter Katie with glorious auburn hair who lived and ran a commercial pig enterprise along the top road. It was good to talk to her about our respective piggy experiences and resulted in the family visiting us for coffee so hubby Paul could give Mick the benefit of his opinion on our set up. It was a lovely visit, Christmas decorations were up and Katie happily settled with biscuits in front of cartoons on the telly whilst we settled around the kitchen table with Paul and Hazel. It was great to learn so much about how to keep happy, healthy free range pigs on a small scale and learn from their experiences. By the end Mick had arranged for loan of one of their new young Tamworth boars for Big Pig at the end of January and he would also stay with us for Little Pigs first run with a boar when she was ten months old.

Waiting for the weather to get better I resorted to making wine with anything I could find in the veg rack and freezer having proved the rack over the range was now just the right warmth for fermentation and a variety of colours in the demijohns made a great display. I ended up with a varied winter selection of: Lemon, Grapefruit, Orange, Banana and Potato all bubbling away atop the range, it would be interesting to see how they turned out.

Our trio of porkers were really getting big and we started to think of them in terms of pork, Mick saw Ab who was of similar opinion for those he had from us and it was agreed that our trio and four of the ones we sold to the college would all travel together in the college trailer for slaughter on 8th January. He was keeping one of our gilts to start a herd, we were that proud! Apparently the abattoir was a small family run one, expert in pig despatch at Tregaron an hour away in the next valley. It was good to know that the pigs would only be having a relatively short journey in familiar transport, ensuring they were as comfortable as possible and minimising stress. Once despatched the carcasses would be collected by the butcher from Llangadog village, nine miles from us, the following day and a week later butchered into neat boxes of joints and chops ready for our collection. Good meat doesn't get much fresher than that!

This was exactly what we had hoped we could achieve, the joy of seeing animals born and providing them with a happy life; free to roam and behave naturally and a stress free quick end resulting in fresh meat for our table with enough left over to hopefully be sold and go towards the costs of looking after them. Whilst not to everyone's taste, pardon the pun; it really brought home the importance of knowing the history of the meat you were eating. First the moral obligation to know the animals had been well treated from conception to birth, a happy unrestricted natural life and stress free despatch, secondly, to not add to the current climate problems, significantly added to by the transporting of foodstuffs, animal and vegetable across thousands of miles.

City work colleagues expressed concern at how we could kill animals we had raised and I agreed we had been worried at how we would deal with it but having seen things almost all the way through I knew I would much rather know the history of what I was eating, how could they happily buy pre packed meat from supermarkets without knowing its history, how had it been conceived, born and looked after? It made them think twice, I was proud that our animals lived naturally without unnatural restriction and became quite obsessed looking at the meat labels in the supermarkets. The sources varied across Europe with the odd Union Jack hidden under the 'half price' joints of the foreign countries. Most laid claim to being 'Fresh' but looking at the list of additives, places of origin and shrink wrapped plastic wrapping I found it hard to believe any of the meat in these cabinets fulfilled the claim. Comparing this to the local butchers window display where local meat deliveries are on sale the same day is like comparing chalk to cheese, here 'Fresh' is exactly that. Enough of moralising, time to return to the real world.

I phoned Les Bailey, the butcher the day after the deed had been done to go through what cuts of meat we wanted and was very happy to be guided by him as we didn't have a clue about how much meat would be involved and what would be the best way to do it. Les was really kind and patiently listened to my naïve ideas. I had this vision of making a range of different flavoured sausages, as and when I fancied from the stock of sausage meat we would have in the freezer, this I was told was not the best of ideas as good sausages required making as soon as the meat had been cut from the carcass to ensure the right consistency to produce succulent well formed sausages. The

Crane Sausage Company idea was shelved for the foreseeable future and Plan B adopted, Les making the sausages using the different flavours I came up with, enabling us to get a good variety of sausages for both our own and hopefully our prospective customers, suffice to not only cover the cost of making but go a bit towards the slaughter/butchery bill we had to add to the cost of keeping the pigs for the six months prior to reaching this stage. That sorted we listed the joints from leg through shoulder to breast together with chops, spare ribs and belly pork ending with liver and kidneys which would be neatly packaged in half pig boxes for our collection the following day. As we finished Les told me our meat was excellent, very lean with just the right amount of fat (a bit like us!), an endorsement of their free range lifestyle, proud as punch I couldn't wait to tell Mick.

That evening was spent trying to work out what meat we should keep and what we should sell, and more importantly at what price to cover the monies we had invested so far. A local had sold a number of butchered pigs a couple of month's back we were told for £150, a price the butcher thought was over the top. Using this as a benchmark, together with the butcher's prices and checking the prices in our local supermarket we decided on £65 for half a pig, £2 for 1lb sausages and £2 per 1lb for the joints and chops. Not the top price but blooming good value for free range lean pork and more importantly if we could sell most of it we would have covered our costs and still have half a pig in the freezer to keep us going until the next lot.

The next morning working from home paid off in that between jobs I was able to ring round a few friends to see if they would be interested in buying any of our pork products, by the end of the day I had managed to sell two half pigs and 5 packs of sausages! Deducting another whole pig, which was to go pal Sue in exchange for her butchered lamb we would be left with one pig of various joints, chops and 51 packs of sausages in the freezer, for sale piecemeal. That afternoon we met Les the butcher at the shop, he really was how you imagined a butcher to look, hale and hearty with twinkling eyes, a great sense of humour and a passion for what he did. One of the pigs was still being prepped and he took great pride in taking us behind the counter to see things for ourselves, showing us the fridge where the carcasses were kept, pointing out the things to look out for which showed how well the meat was, lean or fatty, the right weight for its size, even whether it had been stressed! It was good to hear again that ours were great, if a little on the lean side for his taste. He then showed us the whole cutting process, even showing us how the sausage machine worked before finally revealing six big boxes of pork in various guises and 3 enormous bags of sausages which were all ours, Christmas come early!! We were quite overcome at the excellent result and pathetically grateful to Les for taking the trouble to reassure us that just as much care and attention went to the animals after collection by him as did before by us. Mick and I were also relieved that we both felt the same, bubbling with pride and happy to hear the small abbatoir in Tregaron had a much deserved reputation for looking after the animals and slaughtering as painlessly and quickly as possible.

It was dark as we came back into the valley and stopped at Nerys', our pony friend, our first customer of half a pig. Delivery made, together with our first barter of six duck eggs and a jar of homemade runner bean chutney for a pack of sausages we then called on Sue to drop off her pig meat. Once indoors we set up a sausage packaging line in the kitchen with Mick weighing, me bagging and Tia lying in the middle, intent on tripping us up to get a taster! The sausages were enormous, 100% meat and 5 weighed a pound. The first batch was put straight in the range for a late supper. Helped along by medicinal glasses of cider, an hour later we had a giant pile of bagged sausages and turned our attention to the meat boxes. A quick count of contents showed that one pig produced 13 joints plus tenderloin, 8 bags of four pork chops, four bags of belly pork slices, one very large liver which sliced neatly into four bags and kidneys. Finally all was safely stored in the freezers and we celebrated the results with a very very late supper of our first 'homegrown' sausages topped with three enormous fried duck eggs. The sausages were perfect, so meaty they were worthy of elevation from fry up to roast dinner, complemented by the enormous creamy soft yolks of the duck eggs, bliss! As we dozed on the settee afterwards we felt totally satisfied that we had made the right choice, it was hard work but it was a good life!

From pigs to princes

With perfect timing just as Big Pig came back into season we were loaned a young boar. He was a lovely looking golden Tamworth, perky and well built, as well as well hung, and with a lovely temperament, trouble was he was half the size of Big Pig and we were concerned whether he would be up to the task, despite, as the pig farmer lending him so delicately put it, 'where there's a willy there's a way!' Little Pig safely relocated we let the boar into the sty compound with Big Pig expecting instant action. She unfortunately seemed to have formed the same opinion as us and treated him like one of the kids, tossing him to one side so she could get pole position in the straw. Time would tell, hopefully and she would change her mind and find him attractive, even if Mick needed to build him a ladder to achieve the objective. As sows come into season every three weeks we wouldn't have long to find out.

The back of the sty was now able to double up as a sheep feeding and shelter area, making life easier for Mick as all the feed bins were in there and also saving wear on the paddock around the trough areas. The sheep quickly got used to coming in which also meant we would have an easier job for health checks and maintenance, rather than trying to corner them in the paddock. The new routine was working well until one morning we heard a loud bang, this was repeated with a regularity which made us both look toward the pig pen as it sounded like Big Pig was throwing a wobbly. She however was stood in the doorway with a bemused expression on her face. The banging continued and Mick suddenly started laughing, "bet its Rambo", he called as he went over to investigate. Peering through the window he saw he was right. Rambo was not daft and had planned an assault on the feed bins behind the back door, unfortunately he didn't think it through and having pushed open the door and got in he had backed it shut in his eagerness to get to the feed and couldn't get out. Finding he was not only trapped but also couldn't get the lids of the feed bins to make imprisonment worthwhile he was venting his frustration by charging and butting the door and walls. Mick was about to open the door to let Rambo out when he thought perhaps a little distance was needed between them. A broom handle became the weapon of choice and standing well back Mick prodded the door open. Rambo charged out, snorting and stomping, looking for a victim, determined to assert his authority. The image somewhat destroyed as he now had a fetching white streak across his totally black horns from butting the whitewashed wall. When we had finished laughing we restored his dignity with a handful of lamb nuts, rubbed off the offending paint and he went back to harassing the ewes until they lay down to avoid his attentions.

Despite his posturing, grinning and chasing the girls around we had not seen the deed done but hoped that was because our ewes were good girls and insisting on wooing and doing discretely after dark, well away from prying eyes. After a few months Rambo was leaving the girls alone and we hoped this meant they were all now pregnant. In February our sheep mentors Tony and Margaret came to check them over and confirmed Rambo had earned his keep and all being well we would have our first lambs in the Spring, result!! After giving them all an injection, which would protect them and the lambs from numerous sheep nasties, we celebrated with an extra round of lamb nuts for them and mugs of tea for us.

During February I suffered chronic neck and arm pains brought on not by the outdoor life but by the day job from prolonged use of the computer in poor conditions. The result was I needed an op to replace a disc in my neck to avoid more serious damage to the spinal column. As the surgeon would have to go past the voice box to get to the problem a side effect may be loss of voice for a while, Mick at least was now looking forward to the op! Until then I had to get used to the fact I couldn't sit for longer than 20 minutes in one position without pain. Ironically the 20-minute curfew has now become a rule I apply to everything due to good advice from the unlikeliest source. After the op when receiving physio at the small cottage hospital in Llandovery I was asked if I minded someone sitting in on my next session. Thinking it was just another medical student I had no objections but was surprised to be told not to go to the main entrance but in through the back where a policeman waited with the physio to let me in, my visitor was Prince Charles who was visiting the area having recently purchased a new Welsh home south of Llandovery. There was I sat atop the physio bench, legs swinging and only able to croak as the room filled with local reporters, security and a lady intent on explaining how to greet royalty. Prince Charles was escorted in and shaking my hand chatted about how he suffered from back problems himself and how the best advice he was ever given was from his grandmother who said to never do anything for longer than twenty minutes without a change. Then he showed me a good exercise to try and wished me well for the future, I was smitten, such a caring gentleman. I even had my moment in the spotlight when the visit was shown on the Welsh news that night, there I was legs swinging, chatting to his Royal Highness, albeit for only 30 seconds, I was so proud.

Following a work health assessment I was provided with special work kit to help alleviate the remaining neck and back symptoms and my traveling to London was reduced to once a month, with no working on the computer whilst commuting. Life became so much simpler and less stressful as a result. Mick was now working all day around the holding or renovating the cottage and I worked from home much more, only going down the valley to stock up on food and essentials before heading for home again. Not spending time traveling and in meetings made me much more productive as now having the right IT to hand I was able to respond to jobs much quicker. The only downside was the ability to work and be available 24/7, it took a long while to balance being flexible whilst maintaining a good home balance. Homeworking is definitely not for everyone, I am definitely a convert and would have to be dragged kicking and screaming back into an office environment again. Not having to deal with daily office politics is worth its weight in gold.

Our social life now was a drink and a chat in the garden or kitchen depending on the weather, joined by whoever happened to be passing for eggs and pork, that and the occasional walk up to the pub. Equally gym and other organized fitness classes were redundant as we were continually working out with mucking out, building and gardening. Beauty treatments also a thing of the past, my only concern when going out now was to try and get the dirt out from under my fingernails and make sure there were no nasties on the soles of my shoes. Working from home also greatly reduced my wardrobe. The local charity shops were grateful recipients of my girly going out clothes and high heels, which were now totally redundant. My only clothes criteria now being whether I can climb over fences in it and its suitability for close contact with the pigs.

Lambing live!

My mum and brother Andy were visiting again and having recovered from the eight hour coach journey from Hampshire to Carmarthenshire we went on a tour of the 'grounds' ending with a walk around the paddock watching the now heavily pregnant ewes contentedly grazing. Andy called me up to the top of the slope as he had found a dead lamb, it was really upsetting, even though it wasn't fully formed, and had no fleece you could make out the little hooves. I ran for something to wrap it in and noticed 'Fluffy white' ewe, so named for obvious reasons standing watching us with, a look of bewilderment on her face. She appeared fine and responded well to hand fed nuts before trotting off to join her pals. Nature had obviously decided she was not ready to be a mum yet. After a chat with sheep expert pal Margaret we were reassured that no harm had been done, the miscarriage appeared a one off and there was no reason to think that she would not go to full term next year. It didn't stop us worrying about the others though and binoculars were now permanently kept in the bathroom window, giving us a clear view over the paddock so that we could still keep tabs on them when indoors.

Spring had definitely sprung and it was time to start planting, or at least seeding if I was to keep my end of the bargain and produce vegetables for us. I cleaned out the greenhouse whilst Mick put up stock proof fence and chicken wire around the well-prepped veg patch in anticipation of my success at raising something above ground level. Despite best intentions to do things right I was sidetracked in the planning stage by the Thompson & Morgan seed catalogue which resulted in a vast overspend on a wide variety of packets of seed from multiple varieties of peas and tomatoes to melons and aubergines, the latter not ideal for our Welsh weather. Hindsight is wonderful but as I had the packets I was determined to try for a result and the greenhouse was quickly filled with trays and pots of everything in the seed box and a daily check made to see what would be first to show.

Weekends and late evenings were spent weeding and marking out the veg patch with old planks before planting the potato tubers and onion sets which due to early delivery were so sprouted and tangled I was concerned whether they had any life left to grow anything edible. Happily I was proven wrong, as within weeks they were merrily sprouting, the same couldn't be said of the greenhouse seeds. In fact a month later I resorted to sowing everything direct into the plot leaving only tomatoes and cucumbers to try again in the greenhouse. A good decision as in due course rows of cabbage, sprouts, broad beans, peas and lettuce appeared, followed by leeks, carrots, beetroot and swede. I should add the rows were not always straight and in some cases only populated by one plant, but that was not the point, seeing what the ground was happiest to produce would help me hopefully get it right next year.

As the plants grew so did outside interest, whilst happy to watch the bunnies on the front lawn and the squirrels running along the fence I was not so pleased to see them hopping and bouncing across to the veg patch for a late breakfast. Between these ground assaults, the aerial attacks by the blackbirds and robins and the subterranean sorties by the moles I would be lucky if anything was left for us. The veg patch began to resemble Colditz, fencing supplemented with bricks and blocks along the base, strings of CDs criss crossing the top and kiddies windmills set at strategic points, apparently the wind tremors put off mole. All it needed was me on sentry duty to complete the picture. Just when I thought it couldn't get worse the patch was invaded by blankets of caterpillars; I never even saw a butterfly! Nature was kind I have to say and despite sharing with the wildlife we still ended up with enough veg to keep us going from late June until November. I even harvested the surplus runner beans I had hoped for to build a stock of pickle and chutney. The veg may not have met EU requirements but they definitely met ours and covered the cost of my seed-spending spree.

The weather was starting to warm, but rain was as ever always present in some form or the other. As their fleeces dried the three ewes yet to give birth looked like giant cotton wool puffs. Fluffy white did not seem to have had any bad effects from her miscarriage experience but she had decided she should be the first in line for any attention, wanting to be fed by hand and impatiently pawing at my leg if I didn't oblige quick enough, at least when Tia pawed for food she didn't bruise you!

As lambing became imminent we sought advice from Margaret on the best way forward. As long as the lamb was up and suckling within an hour of birth then all would be well. If the ewe was struggling or gave up trying to give birth after an hour then we were to phone Margaret to come and guide us through an assisted birth. If the lamb wouldn't get up to suckle after an hour we were to feed it substitute colustrum milked from the ewe, or make up a bought substitute and if it didn't respond to again call Margaret to help. It was reassuring to know help would be close if we needed it. Mick made sure the paddock ark was laid with clean straw and a gate set alongside to house anyone needing confining if things didn't go well and we made best use of the binoculars to give us early warning of anything starting. The first sign would be the ewe going off on her own to find a birth site. No signs yet!

On 9th April having just got up Mick called me to the bathroom window, lambing had started without us. Binoculars in hand he showed me our first newborn white lamb, it stood on the slope of the paddock, happily suckling from Black faced ewe, another cunning naming. We quickly dressed and rushed out to check, at a distance, that all was well. No fuss, no mess, just mum and baby getting on with living, like with the piglets births, we felt rather redundant, but in a good way. Watching the lamb's little tail spinning madly, the sign milk was flowing, and mum gently turning to continuing cleaning and nuzzling it closer to the teat. The others kept their distance and we fed the new family separately to give them time to bond. Having survived a night already the lamb was strong on its legs and showing no signs of weakness so we were reassured that it would be safe from any predators. The fox hadn't been seen or smelt in our fields at all and we hoped it stayed that way.

The ewe kept the lamb separate for two days before joining the rest of the flock at the trough. When it lost sight of mum a few distressed bleats soon brought a responding shout and they quickly paired up again. It was amazing how quickly the lamb started to fill out and gain confidence, bleating for mum to come back and let it suckle every couple of hours. It was compulsive viewing and a great timewaster, but it also gave us a practical lesson in what to expect in the future.

A week later when feeding the flock we noticed Raggy Ann, so named because of her dread locked fleece, did not come to the trough and was wandering off on her own, a sign labour was not far off. We carried on with our jobs but kept watch from a distance on how things were progressing. Having settled on her site she started to paw the ground and kept circling before laying down then getting up to repeat the process. Labour was definitely starting and whilst Mick watched I ran for towels, bucket of warm water and lubricant, though as we had been warned only to interfere if there was no other option I hoped none of it would be needed.

By the time I returned Raggy Ann was laid down on her side, lifting her head to the sky and straining, her legs waggled and in one smooth motion out came a big black lamb with a little white tip on its tail. Immediately Raggy started licking it clean and within minutes it had struggled to its feet searching for the teat. We watched in amazement and awe as this little new life, persistently struggled to its feet, drawn to find milk but yet to realise where it was, instinct causing it work its way round mum, ducking under to find the source. Each time the lamb fell mum gently nudged it in the right direction, encouraging with licks and crooning as we held our breath until it finally found a teat and its little tail spun in joy as its first milk was tasted. I found a use for the towel, tears were freely falling, I have never been so close to new life and the overwhelming feeling of happiness was something I would never forget. Mick had developed a cough, which let me know he felt the same, though he would never admit it. We left them in peace to bond without an audience and prayed for a mild night with no predators!

Up at the crack of dawn we saw Raggy Ann grazing with her lamb contentedly laying watching. In the afternoon she brought the babe down to meet the other lamb and resumed feeding at the trough. Encouraged by the others the final ewe, Speckle face, name self explanatory, went into labour just as dusk fell and successfully delivered another black lamb, this time with a white patch on one ear. It was definitely the smallest of the three but the liveliest in getting to its feet and suckling in record time. True to form she kept it to herself for a day before introducing it to the rest of the flock. All births successful, we were able to relax for a while,

Mention should be made that with all the births Rambo was a proper gentleman. Following each birth he wandered over to check on mother, nudging the lamb, then typical male, seemed at a loss to know what else to do and so wandered off for something to eat.

I think whoever was in charge of Welsh weather was smiling on us as only when lambing was safely over did it revert to type and having had a brief Spring respite the heavens darkened, playful breezes turned into gale force winds and we spent hours of fun securing everything in sight but still the next morning finding debris strewn around the garden, buckets, feedbags and branches and god knows where it came from, a hammock sized bra found hanging from the holly tree! The animals seemed oblivious to it all. We were surprised to find the old greenhouse intact but should have kept the thought to ourselves as that night the wind worked itself up into a rage, banging and crashing about before climaxing with a thunderous clap, the sound of tinkling glass followed by complete silence. Well at least we knew what we would be working on tomorrow.

Cautiously peering out the window the next morning, I saw the greenhouse looked mainly intact, great, just a few panes to replace and the rest of the garden looked clear. Hang on, it looked a bit too clear, I must have been dozy, something didn't look right but I couldn't work out what. Looking back and forth I realized there was a gap where the chicken shed was supposed to be. Five of the chucks were stood on the base, looking skywards, totally bewildered, 'where's our house gone?' Going out to investigate we found although the green house had only lost 3 panes the chicken hut was no more, its remains the other side of the 3ft fence in the paddock, laid out like a flat pack awaiting assembly. Scenes from the Wizard of Oz sprung to mind, a mini whirlwind having been the culprit. As we were one chicken short I hoped it wasn't wearing ruby slippers under the wrecked hut, but no she had more sense and had taken refuge in the old pig ark with the lambs. All chucks accounted for we relocated them to temporary hotel accommodation until Mick rebuilt the hut. The security of the block built pigpen and treats of crusty bread soothing their ruffled feathers and quickly restored their spirits. As we left them gathered round breakfast they cackled away like old ladies in a community centre, trying to best each other's stories of the blitz.

Frisky, fleeced and beaten by the weather

A welcome return to fair-weather and Spring was well and truly sprung. Sap was not only rising with the trees if Little Pig's behaviour was anything to go by, trotting about after Mick and Rambo for male attention, ears cocked and eyes wide she shamelessly flirted, spinning in front of them then nuzzling up to them, she was definitely ready to meet little boar. At the end of May she was allowed to join the grown ups over the old pond. Like a greyhound out of the trap she completed three circuits in record time, checking out sleeping and feed arrangements as a priority before catching up with her mum and introducing herself to little boar, who seemed quite pleased at the arrival of a younger model. Mother and daughter, his own 18 – 30 club holiday, hopefully he would be inspired as we were beginning to think females perhaps weren't his thing.

We had been told that if not mated within a year of sexual maturity the girls could become sterile. As the boar had already been with Big Pig for almost three months without a result we needed to know what the problem was and if he didn't produce the goods for Little Pig then we would know he was not up to the job and we would have to think of a plan B.

Sad to say, even with relocation into the old pond to set the mood and Little Pig to sweeten the deal there was not a lot of love action in evidence. Little Boar's heart may have been in the right place but unfortunately nothing else was. We had been kind in giving him extra time to prove himself at the expense of falling behind our pork production calendar, but after five months it was time to call it a day. A compensation deal was struck which saw little, we suspected gay, boar being exchanged for four welsh white weaners, which at three months old would ensure we had pork hampers in another four months time and give us time to decide how we were going to get the girls 'in pig'. We toyed with the idea of getting our own boar as we didn't want to rely on others, but thinking it through it didn't seem cost effective for only two litters a year, the cost of boars feed, housing and extra wear and tear on our limited land outweighing any advantage of instant access.

Grass was now growing quickly and so were the dandelions, blankets of yellow across the garden. Before Mick could decapitate the weeds with the mower I was out with the carrier bag collecting flower heads to make Dandelion wine, which I had yet to taste but had been told was one of the best. I had to keep telling myself that the end result would justify putting up with the awful smell of the flowers at the beginning, it was really rank, not helped by pal commenting that raw they were a diuretic, at least it explained the smell! Six months later I was really pleased I had stuck with it, a complete change, a refreshing light sparkling wine and one I would definitely make large amounts of next year.

Dandelion wine

  2 quarts dandelion flower heads, 3 1bs sugar, 1 lemon, 1 orange, ½ cup strong cold tea, 6 pints boiling water, campden tablet, wine yeast & nutrient.

  Put dandelion flowers, orange & lemon rind and juice with the tea in a plastic bucket. Pour over boiling water, stir and mash, when cool add crushed campden tablet, cover bucket and leave in the warm for 10 days – ignore the smell it's worth it!!

  Strain liquid into clean bucket, stir in sugar, yeast & nutrient, cover and leave for another 3 days in the warm. Strain into demijohn with airlock and leave to ferment, if fermentation is slow add a little sugar after a week or two to jumpstart it, when fermentation has finished leave to clear then bottle. Leave for 6 months but longer really does improve it even more.

  If wine has finished fermenting but not cleared and has a layer of yucky stuff at the bottom rack it into a clean demijohn using a funnel lined with muslin and leave it to clear.

  Our small flock were definitely well established now, lambs duly frolicking, lush new grass being enjoyed almost as much as the rare occasion of over four weeks without rain, the Welsh summer. The only thing getting the adult sheep down was the weight of their fleeces and so Mick phoned around to find someone happy to turn out for such a small number. He was lucky enough to get a local farmer's son who was happy to show us complete novices what was involved. Mick feeding the sheep in the pig pen paid dividends now as he was able to entice them all in enabling them to be caught one at a time for passing to the shearer, who set up shop in the front fenced compound. Mick had laid a big sheet of plywood over the dirt to give a good shearing surface and the electric shears were suspended on a mobile hanger next to the generator just outside the fence. Mick cornered Rambo first and pulled him by the horns to shearer who wrong footed him to rest between his legs. Rambo sat like a grumpy tramp on his first encounter with a barber, within minutes, devoid of fleece Rambo was freed into the paddock to regain his dignity, rather hard to do as now naked his big horns made him look like a rather podgy misshapen pipe cleaner.

Mick practised his catching and turning skills with the remaining ewes with shearer fleecing in record time and twenty minutes later Rambo was joined by the four ewes, looking positively tiny without their fluffy coats. Raggy Ann's name was no longer appropriate, as she looked as svelte and pristine as Black face who had similar markings. They bounced round happily enjoying the weight loss, the lambs chasing them, trying to work out who belonged to who as the removal of mums fleeces also removed a lot of their smell. After a madcap game of chase around the paddock the ewes came to their senses and as the lambs bleated they returned to their respective offspring, letting them suckle before resting with them nuzzled close, order returned once more.

We then had a lesson in how to roll the fleeces and stacked them in the sty to keep dry. Whilst striving for self-sufficiency I did not think the potential yarn from five fleeces would justify the work and equipment needed to get it to a useful stage. A simple solution was to donate it to our neighbours, the Coleg, whose craft workers were pleased to have coloured fleeces to work with, it was also a way of saying thank you to Ab the Coleg farm manager for all his advice and help.

Rambo stayed at the top of the bank for the rest of the day, striking heroic poses and trying to reassert his masculinity, rather difficult in his shorn state but come feed time at the trough he used his horns to good effect and due respect was given by the girls.

The men relaxed with a welcome glass of cider whist I turned my attention to making yet more wine. Sue had a glut of Rhubarb which she had kindly shared with me as my newly planted crown was far off producing the large old sticks needed for the wine recipe, a much better use than just throwing them on the compost heap. Keeping the demijohn and bottles wrapped in paper make sure it keeps a lovely pink colour and when finished it becomes a really tasty rose'.

Rhubarb wine

3lb Rhubarb, 3lb sugar, 6 pints boiling water, campden tablet, pectic enzyme, yeast & nutrient.

3lb Rhubarb cut in small pieces and put in bucket with sugar and boiling water, stir until dissolved, cover, leave to cool, add crushed campden tablet, pectic enzyme, cover and leave for 24 hours. Stir in yeast & nutrient, cover, and leave in warm for 7 days stirring daily. Strain into demijohn with airlock and ferment. When clear bottle – drink after 6 months, but leave a bottle or two to get even better!

Finally we got planning permission for our biggest outbuilding project, a store/garage across the lane from the workshop. Our pride and joy the VW camper had been living in the garden for two years and was desperately in need of a good home, as were all the other mechanical bits and pieces stored in our dilapidated sheds. The building was to have its back to the lane and face out over the valley, with a good outside maintenance area. With such a lovely view across the river and the benefit of the camper over there I would know where Mick was whenever he went AWOL.

At last a decent dry spell saw the reforming of the concrete laying team, Mick, Pete and Les to lay the concrete base, made a lot easier by having the concrete delivered ready mixed and poured for them to level. Despite the delivery being ¼ short, which meant frantic preparation of a new mix with our small mixer to fill the gap before the ready poured set and the heavens opened again, the team completed with minutes to spare. Mick's working days got longer and longer as he tried to make sure the building was up and wind and watertight before .the end of the year. The concrete blocks were really weighty and it was a job in itself just trying to get them where he needed them, getting harder the higher up he got. Trying to load them onto the borrowed scaffolding trestle and then up onto the next course really took its toll. My feeble efforts to help ended as soon as he left ground level. The scale seemed immense compared to the pigpen, but like a Duracell bunny Mick wouldn't quit and managed to finish the block work before the weather broke. No mean feat as the building was 20ft square and over 14 ft high. Mick only stopped when rain and winds set in for the duration and he resigned himself to leaving the roof and doors until the weather improved.

Although wet the summer temperature continued to rise and

we now had the perfect conditions for other sheep nasties to start, like fly strike and lameness. For light relief from building work Mick reverted to shepherd and with Tia and myself ably assisting, corralled the flock for a foot check and drench. Rambo first, the battle of wills as to who would end up on their bum was epic. Mick did win but needed five minutes to recover before he could start the job. Then it was the ewes' turn, much easier to work with he rolled them to sit contentedly between his legs. To spare Mick's already aching back I became the hoof trimmer while he held them. There was a real knack to cleaning out any gaps between hoof and pad before trimming any overgrown bits back to an even level. Armed with the antiseptic spray I did manage to complete with only one nick drawing blood which had no effect on the ewe, she was more annoyed at the bright blue spray now covering one foot. All finished and duly dosed for worms and drenched with a multi purpose fly protection liquid they were let back onto the paddock to hopefully enjoy good health for the foreseeable future. As I was in London for business meetings the next day I spent a pleasant half hour getting rid of the blue stain from my hands, always a conversation stopper in polite company.

It proved a job well done as the rain which started in earnest at the beginning of July didn't stop until August, varying only in intensity from gentle drizzle to monsoon. The paddock, although waterlogged was still firm enough for animals; the old pond was a different story. As the pigs had rooted around they had managed to puddle clay together so it was holding water at one end, and like the tide coming in, as the heavens opened they were waking not to views of grass but waterfront, gently lapping at the front door with squatters in the form of a pair of ducks and a heron playing statue in the middle, like a giant garden ornament. After moving the ark further back onto firm dry ground, three times in two weeks with no sign of the rain abating and even less of the ground recovering before Autumn it was time to admit our land management plan had been defeated and move the girls back into the pigpens.

The continual rain together with the loss of long days meant resigning ourselves to shelving any further outbuilding plans and making the most of any brief dry spells to try and reduce the muddy swamps between the animal compounds to a level that we could safely walk on without sinking knee deep in foul mud and losing our wellies. There is nothing more frustrating than when being trapped knee deep in mud you finally manage to pull one foot up out of the smelly sucking mess only to find your foot bereft of sock and welly, do you a) put it straight back in and shout for help, only to remember other half has gone out, resign yourself to a long wait and immediately need the loo, or b) accept your foot will never be the same and boldly hope as you stride out that you don't sink further, your toes don't meet anything wriggly and that your other foot does join you or you end up back at a) bereft of wellies but also with your legs pointing in opposite directions and you hoping desperately help arrives before you have to give in and sit down! Having had the latter happen I was now a fan of running boards, any old lengths of wood strategically placed to help keep us out of the mire.

Despite the rain the raspberry canes were fruiting on a daily basis and this would continue until the end of August. I was on a daily quest to pick them before ruined by rain or pinched by the birds sneaking through the netting. There were quite a few wild raspberry canes in the hedges which although tiny did add to the bounty. Each day's pickings were added to a carrier bag in the freezer which after two months resulted in enough to make 8 jars of jelly and 24 bottles of wine, a great way to spend a rainy day and provided just enough to keep us going until next year. Raspberry wine is full bodied and fruity, a great substitute for Cabernet Sauvignon and the jelly whilst great on toast and scones is also brilliant with chicken or turkey instead of cranberry.

Raspberry Jelly

4lb raspberries, 1lb cooking apples, juice of 1 lemon, 1 ¼ pints water, ¾ lb sugar per pint of juice made

Cut apples in quarters (leave on skin and don't core), put in saucepan with the water and lemon juice and cook until pulpy. Add the raspberries and stew until soft. Strain juice through muslin, you can leave it overnight to drip or if impatient like me squeeze the muslin bag (or clean tight leg!!) to get as much out as possible.

Sterilise jam jars and a glass jug then dry in the oven so they are warm when you are ready to use them. Measure the juice to work out how much sugar you want then heat the juice in a saucepan, add the sugar and stir until dissolved. Bring to the boil and boil quickly for eight minutes then test it will set by dipping in a cold spoon, if on cooling it coats the spoon, goes sticky and wrinkles when pushed then it will set. Add a small knob of butter and stir to remove any scum, this means you don't lose any jelly, you can remove any scum with a slotted spoon instead.

Pour into warm jug then into jars, filling to the top, cap with greaseproof paper rounds then put on lids loosely, tighten when cool.

Raspberry wine

3 ½ lb raspberries, 3lb sugar, 6 pints boiling water, campden tablet, pectic enzyme, yeast & nutrient.

Put raspberries, sugar and water in bucket stirring until dissolved. Cover and when cool add crushed campden tablet and pectic enzyme, cover for 24 hours. Add yeast & nutrient, cover and leave in warm for 10 days. Strain liquid into demijohn with airlock, keep warm and ferment. When clear bottle, rack first if there is a lot of sediment in the demijohn. Very nice in 6 months, but even better if left longer.

Any red wine should be kept in the dark to keep its colour; brown paper round the bottle will also do the job.

Juggling sheep

Despite the rain the lambs were full of the joys of the summer; filling out nicely they had both milk and grass to keep them content. Watching them was a great timewaster, especially when they played at dusk and went completely bonkers, jumping on their mum's and Rambo's backs as they dozed then having roused them racing off up to the top of the paddock to see who could jump on top of the old felled tree trunk first. The winner then had to fight off the others as they tried to be the new king of the castle. Their play was infectious and it wasn't long before the adults were joining in with gusto. Just like kids there were always 'tears before bedtime', normally in the form of Rambo deciding it was time to call a halt by gaining possession of the top of the log, head and horns well down, a great deterrent to the rest who knowing when it was time to quit quietly wandered off to find a patch for the night.

The ewes would come in season once the nights started to draw in and traditionally tupping, courting to you and me, began on Bonfire Night when the ram was left with the ewes, this would ensure lambs born in good weather in Spring. As the lambs were doing so well and ready to be weaned Mick decided to separate them with Rambo so that the ewes could enjoy a couple of months on their own to let them be fully rested and hopefully more than happy to welcome Rambo's attentions again later in the year.

Using the main pigpen for a stress free split, all sheep went in for a good feed then Rambo and the lambs were let out the front and enticed with a bucket of lamb nuts into the front enclosure with fresh grass whilst the ewes were let back on the paddock. For the next few days the lambs and ewes called for each other but this seemed more for reassurance than need. They were all ok, watching or talking to each other through the fence the lambs soon settled into looking after themselves. Rambo kept the lambs in order and they quickly learnt to jump out of his way when he decided to have a back scratch using the sides of the ark or wanted pole position at the water trough.

The only thing growing now in the greenhouse were the marigolds, they had taken over, having finished the job of protecting the tomatoes from unwanted insects they were now enormous bushes of beautiful smelling flowers which I couldn't bear to see wasted and so unsurprisingly I found a recipe for Marigold wine. Adding those found in the veg bed I had more than enough to make 2 demijohns. Like the flowers the wine was a lovely golden amber colour, a real taste of late summer.

Marigold wine

4 quarts marigold flowers, 3lb sugar, 1lemon & orange, ½ cup strong cold tea, 6 pints boiling water, campden tablet, wine yeast & nutrient.

Put flowers, lemon and orange rind & juice, cold tea and boiling water in a bucket, stirring and mashing, when cool add crushed campden tablet. Cover and leave for 4 days, strain liquid into saucepan and heat to boil then pour over sugar in clean bucket, stir until dissolved, when cool add yeast and nutrient. Cover, leave in warm for 3 days stirring daily, strain into demijohn with airlock and leave in warm until fermentation has finished, bottle, drink after 6 months, or longer.

It was Mick's birthday at the end of September and this coincided with his decision to get another two ewes. When I heard the van arrive back I assumed he had arranged for Tony to deliver the sheep later in the week and so was taken by surprise to see him walk past the window carrying a bemused looking sheep. Running out to open the first enclosure gate for him before his arms gave out he gently put the sheep down, telling me it was easier to bring them back in the van, nicely cushioned with bales of straw and went back to the van for another one. The first one lay where placed, eyes fixed on me, still as a statue, not a twitch. Sheep's eyes are really disconcerting, fixed in a mad stare and you have no chance of knowing what they are thinking. I gently scratched her behind the ear and trance broken she was upright and away to munch grass in a flash. Mick had a similar result with the other one. A year younger than our girls they were the same breed, both black faced with similar markings but one had one ear tag and the other two, so they were suitably named Birthday Girl One and Birthday Girl Two.

We let them get their bearings and fed them in the small enclosure where they would stay for the night before joining the other ewes on the paddock in the morning. Curiosity drew the rest of the flock to see who was getting priority treatment. The two groups lined along the fences didn't faze the new girls who feigning indifference just carried on munching, but with one eye and both ears cocked for any reason to take flight. Let into the paddock with the rest of the ewes the next day they kept themselves separate for a while but come feeding time they slowly worked things out and pecking order established joined the others at the trough, taking with a pinch of salt being butted out if they overstepped the mark. Within a week they had bonded into one small flock all looking out for each other, Raggy Ann mentoring one and Speckle face the other. It took a while longer for them to take food by hand, but that was mainly due to the others getting there first.

September also saw the best blackberry season yet and I was spoilt for choice both in the hedgerows and down in the Crusher. Blackberry jelly was a firm favourite for breakfast toast but I also liked Blackberry wine so I was really chuffed to be able to collect huge amounts for both. Tia was in two minds about blackberry picking, on the one hand she got lot longer walks and was able to wander about following scents of rabbit and fox whilst I picked, on the other she got bored sitting around waiting for me if there was nothing else to keep her interest. It didn't take long to harvest so much that not only did the pantry become well stocked with wine and jars of jelly but the freezer held enough for more making sessions when the weather was too bad to do anything else.

Blackberry and apple jelly

4lb blackberries, 1lb cooking apples, uice of 1 lemon, 1 ¼ pints water, ¾ lb sugar per pint of juice made

Cut apples in quarters (leave on skin and don't core), put in saucepan with the water and lemon juice and cook until pulpy. Add the blackberries and stew until soft. Strain juice through muslin – you can leave it overnight to drip or if impatient like me squeeze the muslin bag (or clean tight leg!!) to get as much out as possible.

Sterilise jam jars and a glass jug then dry in the oven so they are warm when you are ready to use them. Measure the juice to work out how much sugar you want then heat the juice in a saucepan, add the sugar and stir until dissolved. Bring to the boil and boil quickly for eight minutes then test it will set by dipping in a cold spoon, if on cooling it coats the spoon, goes sticky and wrinkles when pushed then it will set. Add a small knob of butter and stir to remove any scum, this means you don't lose any jelly, you can remove any scum with a slotted spoon instead.

Pour into warm jug then into jars, filling to the top, cap with greaseproof paper rounds then put on lids loosely, tighten when cool.

Blackberry wine

3lb blackberries, 3lb sugar, 6 pints boiling water, campden tablet, wine yeast & nutrient, pectic enzyme.

Put blackberries and boiling water in bucket stirring in sugar until dissolved, cool, add pectic enzyme and crushed campden tablet, leave for 24 hours covered in a warm place. Add yeast & nutrient, leave for seven days in the warm. Strain into demijohn with airlock, leave to ferment then bottle.

Leave for 6 months and you have a lovely deep ruby red sweet wine, ideal with chocolate or hot with spice.!

Tupping time and pleasuring pigs!

From the behaviour of Rambo it was clear the ewes were all giving off signals that they were available. He spent best part of the day striking heroic poses along the fence, raising his magnificent head to the sky and curling his top lip back in a cheesy grin which was a preliminary to him wanting to get a bit closer to his intended. To ensure they were all fighting fit Mick gave them all a check over, trimming any overgrown hooves so they didn't cause any damage in the games ahead. Happy they were all healthy and ready to rock and roll, Rambo was let back into the paddock and the lambs moved onto the final fresh grass in the run alongside the paddock, well out of the way of any adult shenanigans.

In their second year the older girls were expected to produce twins and in their first the Birthday Girls to have singles. Rambo made a beeline for Fluffy White, who despite giving him the come on was just as quick to wander off when he followed up his cheesy grin with a pawing of her side and rump, she was obviously playing hard to get. Not wishing to be total voyeurs we left them to it.

Fluffy White having aborted in her first year was an unknown, we had resisted some opinions that we should have got rid of her as we weren't in this commercially so as far as we were concerned she was with us for good. Even if she didn't lamb again, she was a real character, a bit of a loner she was always following me round, pawing at my leg for the lamb nuts she knew were always in my pocket and the first to get to the trough, but also the first to leave, obviously watching her weight. Her fleece in the winter was spectacular, a giant white puffball, she'd never suffer from cold or lack of padding, she was obviously Rambo's favourite which maybe explained why she thought she was a bit above the rest, with her haughty but naughty come hither wiggle she was the sheep equivalent to Mae West.

Now the sheep reproduction cycle was in no doubt our thoughts turned back to how to secure pig pregnancies as soon as possible. After lengthy debate we decided to try artificial insemination with Big Pig. Made confident by talking online with pedigree pig producers who on being told of our small boar requirements and limited land recommended it as the best option, simple and productive with minimum stress caused to the sow. Following their advice I phoned the experts, Deerpark in Ireland, who were the UK supplier of pedigree boar semen by first class post together with tools and instructions on how to do the job. One very practical and informative conversation later and I was convinced this might work, £25 seemed a small price to pay for a litter of piglets without the need for a boar, though given the choice I didn't think Big Pig would agree!

We soon found out. An order was made as soon as Big Pig came in season. The next morning the postman stood at the gate with a cheeky smile on his face holding a polystyrene box and four very long thin plastic tubes which looked like catheters with rubber corkscrews on the end. I was quick to explain their purpose to avoid any rumours which this delivery might have caused about strange goings on at the Crane place, and he fell about laughing at the thought of what the weird things were actually for. For the delicate ones amongst you I wont go into gory details other than to say the box contained three bottles of the liquid to go in the tubes which in turn were gently inserted in the obvious place, and yes a male pig's parts do end in a corkscrew, adding a whole new meaning to the phrase 'screwing around'.

The theory was for 'Boarmate' spray, irresistible boar scent, to waft in front of Big Pig's nose causing her to stand still waiting for the act to be done. This would be repeated for three days and three weeks later, if there was no sign of her being in season we would have a pregnant pig, how quick, how simple, how wrong! I assumed as helper I would be at Big Pig's head with the spray and Mick, surrogate boar, would be at the tail end, no way, when he realised what was involved in getting things in the right place he decided I could deal with the business end and he would talk dirty at the front. I guess the female always has a better chance of finding the right spot. Big Pig was invited into the compound, Mick doing his best boar imitation, trousers on I hasten to add, spray duly tempting her to stand still. So far so good, as he talked to her reassuringly I loaded the long catheter tube and lifting her tail, making sure I was in the right place, managed to screw into position and start gently pumping in the semen, pandemonium, Big Pig realised she had been conned, wanted a boar, not a sex toy and with a speed belying her bulk took off round the compound with me in pursuit trying to retrieve the catheter swinging madly behind her spraying me with its contents, suffice to say it took me half an hour to clean my glasses! Mick was also suffering but only because his stomach hurt from laughing so much.

None the worse for her experience Big Pig, once she had calmed down, wandered back for a scratch, I removed the offending foreign object and we withdrew leaving her to a late breakfast, rather than a post coital cigarette. We left it until the afternoon to try again, this time no bolting, but a gentle wandering around with me holding the tube up, determined to empty the bottle, even though half ended up on my wellies. Third time lucky the next morning saw the third bottle emptied but from Big Pig's lack of involvement and loss of much of the bottle contents we weren't confident. One thing it did do was making up our minds that the girls deserved the real thing, but how to get it?

Bang on cue, in catching up with Ab on how the sow we had sold him was doing we were pleased to hear he had just purchased a proven boar, which having laughed himself silly at our AI story, he would be happy for us to borrow at the end of November, for two seasons, six week. This should see Big and Little Pig in pig and save Ab six weeks feed and mucking out. Predictably named Boris, a Tamworth, the boar was said to be very gentle, somewhat contrary to the fact that his handler had been in hospital for the last three weeks after two ops to repair the muscle damage done to his arm by Boris's tusks when he naively tried to take two of his piglets out of his sty. Noting our concern, Ab kindly said he would come back with us when we picked the boar up to see everything went smoothly.

Four weeks later and with both Big and Little Pig clearly in season we collected Boris without incident with the quad bike pulling the trailer along the rough track between our respective holdings. Boris bouncing happily in the back and me jumping on and off to open the field gates in-between. The only hold up being the final big field with the cows and bull in who having been interested when we went through the first time were now crowded around the gate expecting a feed and instead got a mad female shouting loudly, waving arms like a windmill and advancing on them to get them away from the gate. Luckily they decided to run away before I did and we crossed safely, pulled onto our paddock and up to the pigpen.

Boris was loud and lively as Ab and Mick opened the trailer door and he rushed out to meet the girls, who we hoped would respond with a flirty display at best and demure acceptance at worse, not a chance. One look at the rampant sex machine and they both started screaming, increasing the volume every time Boris so much as looked in their direction. By the time he started to try it on the pitch was unbearable. Despite Ab's reassurance that this was normal as he was invading their territory and it would settle down, I couldn't stand it, my girls were distressed and I didn't like it and went indoors. Apparently they were a lot less upset than I was and within twenty minutes screaming had subsided and the fun had begun.

By morning they were all curled up contentedly together and it was evident that they were now a happy ménage a trois, with the exception of mealtimes when it was every pig for himself or herself. We were so pleased as they would be confined to barracks for the next six weeks to let Boris do what he did best and hopefully leave them both with early Christmas presents.

Inspired by the fully stacked wood shed and vast amount of fallen timber around after the gales Mick decided we would convert the range back to wood and discontinue the oil until prices were more sensible. High already as the weather got colder they shot through the roof and despite our best efforts to reduce our use we were facing over £2000 a year just for heating and cooking. Every spare hour was now spent collecting, chopping and stacking supplies of wood to feed the range and the two wood burners through till next Spring. Juggling the range heat was the biggest challenge, especially on Sunday evenings, trying to get the water hot enough for two baths at the same time as producing enough heat for roast potatoes, I failed miserably and resorted to deep frying the spuds, hardly Nigella but at least crispy and on time. Wood burning also increased the time spent on housework, producing a constant layer of wood ash over every surface; still at least I could see where I've been. Most people get more lethargic and put on weight during the colder months. We were more active, chasing wood to feed the three fires from one end of the cottage to the other and lost weight, a definite bonus as we approached the festive season well prepared for over indulgence.

Lambs come of age

The three lambs were now more fat sheep and as the weather was turning for the worst we decided that it was time they went before the roads became really icy. The abattoir started work as soon as the vet arrived to monitor everything and they allotted each load its own arrival time so that the animals had minimal waiting time before it was their turn, so reducing stress at the unfamiliar surroundings. Neil the owner kindly gave us an early slot, 7.30 a.m. as it meant that there would be less chance of any delays from earlier arrivals. Les the butcher was to collect and produce the meat for us for collection just over a week later. Fresh lamb in the freezer for Christmas, excellent! Arrangements made we turned to the practicalities.

As the lambs would be leaving the holding they had to be tagged showing our flock number and an individual tagging number. The tagging device looked like an office hole punch, into which the tag slotted and once pushed together joined the tag around the ear. The plan was for Mick to hold the lamb while I pierced its ear, sounded simple, and having pierced ears myself I hoped it would be as painless for them as it had been for me. It all went very well, I had psyched myself up to not fanny about and to do it as firmly and quickly as possible, still the little crunch noise as the punch pierced through made me cringe, but with a quick shake of the head the lambs happily trotted off back to grazing without any ill effect, showing off their new 'jewellery', nicely placed mid ear with the loop of the tag below to minimize it catching on anything untoward. Mission accomplished, we felt justly proud of the results.

Walking up the lane to church I met around twenty rogue sheep, taking 'free range' to the extreme grazing anything they could get to. They were rounded up by their owner twice a year but otherwise left to wander the valley as the fences and hedges around their fields were easily breached and as we all know the grass is always greener on your own land if you let your sheep graze everybody else's on the other side. They took no offence at being turned and gently escorted off the premises as they simply moved to another freebee, bearing left down to the camp site where the grass was plentiful and as shut for the season they could graze in peace. Rain stopped play for the rest of the day. Torrential hail showers punctured by short bursts of sunshine created spectacular rainbows, which arched across one side of the valley to the other. We had a perfect view from the sitting room that has windows facing both sides of the valley; it was like watching two different days at once. The sheep seemed oblivious, heads down, advancing in formation as they munched their way across the paddock. The three lambs were equally unperturbed, as Mick had let them have the fresh grass in the garden. They were on a mission, trying to eat every item in the flower borders instead, safe in the knowledge we were too warm and cosy to venture out and stop them, the only thing they leave is the mint, still they'll get plenty of mint sauce soon.

Mick had lit the kitchen range early so our pork joint could cook long and slow and also heat up the water so we could celebrate another day without using the immersion heater, he took it as a personal affront if we had to use it, a slur on his fire making! The weather decided us on a lazy day in the front room and so the log burner there was duly lit and we were now feeling that wonderful sense of warm contentment that a real fire brings, listening to the hail outside and dozing on and off as we watched films we had taped months earlier but had no chance to watch. Serendipity was all too short, the quickly reducing daylight hours meant that we soon had to kickstart ourselves to don working clothes and start the afternoon rounds with the animals. Not that you can ever forget the time when you have pigs, they gently remind you that feeding time is imminent with gentle grunting and snorting, quickly changing to ear splitting screams of annoyance if you are more than five minutes late. That had the domino effect of starting the lambs calling for their share, ewes and Rambo joining in followed by the chickens doing what chickens do best, squawking and running after whoever looks like getting the first bucket of feed.

As the main animal carer Mick had feeding time down to a military exercise, on the days I helped I just seemed to manage to sabotage the operation by being in the wrong place with the wrong feed and wrong amounts at the wrong time. Hence my relegation to looking after the chickens, who he has little patience with as he says they seem completely brainless and incapable of listening to him, I resent the insinuation that so am I but scuttled off to track them down from their various hiding places and get them to safety before darkness descends and the fox is on the prowl, hunting is sparse elsewhere and they would be an easy target.

Keeping the lambs happy in their final week was uppermost in our minds. Mick moved the trailer into the little compound and bedding it snugly with straw started giving the lambs a final feed in there, letting them stay in for the night so they were used to going up and down the ramp and being in the trailer in preparation for their imminent early morning trip to Tregaron on 1st December.

To get to the abattoir on time we would need to leave by 6 a.m and as this would be our first trip, the state of the road in the dark could be a problem so we decided to be up by 5.a.m. The night before Mick hitched the trailer to the tractor and brought it round to the front drive where he backed it into the garden and transferred it to the back of the van before checking the trailer board lights were all working in preparation for the journey the next day. We then filled out all the required paperwork, in triplicate and left it next to the mobile phone and torch on the table. An early night followed by an even earlier morning start saw us up, loaded and on the road by quarter to six. Stars lit our way as we slowly made our way out of the valley. Just over an hour later we reached Tregaron, it was almost light and we easily found Neil's place just outside the village, off a single-track access to a number of industrial units, the abattoir being the first one. It looked just like a normal single storey workshop, no scary noises or nasty smells. At the far end was the lairage, the pens where the animals were held before they went through to slaughter; there were only three so it was reassuringly obvious the animals were given quick attention.

As we pulled in the gate a man in white coat waved us forward and asked for our papers, we filled in the arrival time and he disappeared in the office to fill in the receipt details before giving us back a copy for our records. A trailer in front was just pulling out and we were waved forward to reverse up to the lairage to unload our lambs. As the ramp was lowered they trotted out and were guided by the herdsman straight through the door to the main building, by the time we put the ramp up they had been dispatched, no chance for long or even short goodbyes, we couldn't believe how quick it was.

Chatting to the guys doing everything we were really pleased to see how much they cared for the animals and how quick the operation was so that the animals had minimal stress. We both felt surprisingly good, having now seen things through from beginning to end, knowing what a good life the lambs had had and more importantly knowing they had been treated well through to the end. Now we looked forward to our meat hampers in a fortnight, we had already agreed sale of one whole butchered lamb, leaving two for our freezer.

The big freeze

Temperatures dropped below freezing adding more chores. Breaking ice on all water troughs in the morning and as the garden tap and pipes were frozen up making sure all available buckets were filled the night before and stored in the green house to stop the water freezing. The sun shone brightly from noon till three when it dipped again and we lost the light by four. One good thing coming of this reduced outdoor time was that the chucks no longer had to be persuaded to go home for the night, they were all indoors by dusk, giving us longer evenings to relax and turn attention to indoor jobs put off for too long. Sorting out the pile of paperwork relating to the animals was high on the list to be ready for any audit by DEFRA and any other organisation policing smallholders. One good result of the frozen conditions was that the muddy impassable swamp that the pigpens had become was solid enough to walk on without fear of being stuck there for the rest of the day.

The gang of four white porkers in the ark slept one atop the other to maximise body heat. We kept topping up the straw to give them a cosy nest but the beggars were so active that it was quickly reduced from a thick duvet to a thin mat. We realised the increased activity in the ark was due to the boars testosterone kicking in resulting in them trying to mount anything in sight giving off any faint female pig smell. This was confirmed when Little Pig wandered outside their fence whilst in season and one of the little boars launched himself through the gap between the barb wire atop the stock fence to land on her back. A tremendous feat, but landing in the wrong place saw him vainly going through the motions from completely the wrong end!

A quick rethink of housing and a cunning plan was devised to solve the problem. Following Boris's departure the week before Christmas it was decided that the girls would all be housed together, the two white gilts moving into the pigpen with the big girls. This would prevent the young boars bothering them and we would also delay their departure until it was certain that the big girls were in pig. If they weren't then the white gilts would stay and the big girls would go, either way a result would be known by the end of February which was when we estimated the litters would be due. By this time the white gilts would be nine months old and very good size porkers or by eleven months ready to mate with Boris. Mick made the feed pen into a bedsit for the young girls by putting in shelves to hold the feed bins safely out of their reach. Big girls retained the other pen and the large area for wandering in. They settled in quickly, swapping gossip through the gate.

The boys were to go at the end of January so for their remaining four weeks to focus their frustrated energy and spare the swampy run Mick decided to relocate them to my stock proofed veg patch, which was woefully lacking in any veg other than the rotting remains of runner beans, marrow plants, sprout stumps and a few sad leeks, piggy heaven. As with the lambs to reduce stress we decided that the trailer would become their temporary home, opening onto their daytime playground. Everyone was a winner, relocation keeping the girls out of sight and of mind and giving the boys not only a dry cosy bedroom which they would be happy to travel in but also the joy of earthing up the veg patch with all the roots and other piggy treats rather than the dead mess they had created in the other run. Their joy was plain to see as they bounced about from one patch to the other grunting with excitement at each new find, then fighting for the best bits. Even more importantly I would end up with a nicely turned over veg patch for the next season, which would need no digging and be weed free!

That evening Mick simply opened the trailer door onto the veg patch, put a well sprung bed of straw at the back, water trough at the front, then put the feed in, the boys were in like a shot, we shut the door and left them in peace for the night. Routine was quickly established whereby boys were seen to first, door opened, food in veg patch and there they stayed for the day. Big girls were then fed in the large pen, then white gilts in their pen before it was the sheeps' turn in troughs at the back of the sty next to the bank leading up the paddock. A quick walk round the paddock with Tia checking boundaries was enough time for all to have finished feeding and Mick then opened the sty to let the girls onto the paddock for the rest of the day, then let them back in at dusk for evening feed. The new living arrangements resolved any battle of the sexes, though we did like to think this may be because Boris had done his job and the big girls were in pig so they held no interest for the young boars anymore and that the gilts were too young to worry about such things. Still, better safe than sorry.

The sheep quickly learnt to finish their food ahead of the piggy girl gang steaming through the doors to pinch anything left in the troughs, bouncing any slow eaters out of the way. Having had breakfast rudely interrupted the sheep went back to grazing, only to be chased by the gilts trying to get them to play, but they simply stood with a look of amusement on their faces, like grown ups watching the children. The gilts quickly bored of their non response and made for Tia who was more than happy to play chase and rough house with them, even fetching sticks to play tug of war with, though one growl from her if they started to win and they were off like a shot leaving her to chew the offending stick that had let her down. The big pigs, like Rambo, kept a dignified distance but were quick to step in to enforce the pecking order, especially if the gilts were making a fuss of us, they charged over knocking them aside and like minders stopped them coming back, as if to say, 'hands off they're ours!'

Big Pig, the matriarch grandly ambled wherever she wanted and everyone moved round her, she tolerated Little Pig much as a queen would her lady in waiting. Content for her to be close to her at all times but to know her place and defer when food or a good scratch were proffered. Little Pig treated the gilts in the same way, a bit like the class sketch with John Cleese and the two Ronnies. This seemed to suit all concerned, as there was space to run around and escape conflict.

The gilts made the most of the new freedom to roam but were always ready for a nap midday. At first getting them in for the night was bedlam. It started well, with Mick calling them in and the girls making for home as fast as they could to be first to the grub. Trouble was the gilts were much faster than Big and Little pig so arriving ahead they ran straight through to the bigger girls area and started on their feed, seconds later to be cornered by the returning bulk of the big girls who tossed them out screaming blue murder at the mistreatment. Mick putting back the pens dividing board and feeding them in their area by the door quickly calmed them. Showing how intelligent pigs are, the following evening the gilts arrived home first but waited outside until the big girls caught up and had gone through to their trough and Mick shut them off with the dividing board before they went in. Turning to close them all in for the night Mick saw the gilts had been joined by Black Faced ewe, doing her best, albeit totally failing, pig impression she was standing her ground at the trough and pinching their grub. So determined was she to get her fill that Mick had to pick her up and kicking and cursing him carry her outside. Door securely shut, she wandered off up the paddock to plan her next break in.

The added benefit of being able to let the pigs out of the pens was that there was no mucking out to do, they quickly organised their affairs so that the first stop for all of them once out was 'the ladies' area they chose and all stuck to. It was funny to watch them almost queuing to use the same spot in their now agreed pecking order.

Happy Christmas, eventually!

Traditionally Christmas and Boxing Day were the two days of the year when we hibernated, not leaving the settee except for essentials, food, drink, more food, more drink, you get the picture. We had adapted this much loved and well earned routine to include seeing to the animals three times a day and keeping the log basket full. I finished my chores; saucepans of veg lined up on the top of the range and turkey cooking slowly in the bottom, duly stuffed and wrapped up in bacon. Mick got a roaring fire going and enough logs to see it well stocked for the rest of the day and armed with mugs and chocolates we reclined the settee and in the warm with tree lights gently twinkling totally relaxed and sunk into lethargy, bliss!

After an hour or so we restocked the fire, changed our mugs for glasses and I retrieved the presents from under the tree ready for opening when we had the energy, at this rate probably Boxing Day. Gently dozing as we watched (again) the Good Life Christmas Special Mick turned the sound down as he could hear a weird noise outside. Opening the French doors we heard a really loud crackling, like gunfire, which he quickly realized was not over the firing range but the top of our chimney that was on fire! Instant activity, like a bad Laurel and Hardy sketch Mick shot off in one direction to find a ladder, I in the other to roll out a hose, tripping over it as I did so and then finding it was too short, off again for the extension. Mick scrambled up to the roof, hose in hand, I turned on tap and the jet of water hit the chimney cowl where flame was spurting out in both directions. Hot cowl, cold water, loud crack and lots of smoke, Mick disappeared in the cloud for a few minutes before descending black faced to get a rope with which in his best cowboy impression he lassoed the cowl and pulled it off the chimney, which, smashing on the ground revealed that the fire had been caused by debris in the top of it. Disaster averted, cold, wet and smoke charred we went back indoors. A quick clean up, fire confined to the grate and chimney none the worse, Christmas cheer restored we settled down again.

On my next refreshment foray I roused Mick to open the presents I had piled next to where we were sat. As he brought the recliner upright it pierced a badly disguised present, a 3 litre plastic bottle of cider which exploded, spinning madly and spraying everywhere as he tried to catch it and I opened the French doors again so it could be thrown out to join the broken chimney cowl. We could have done with this happening an hour earlier to douse the chimney fire. Anyhow, determined to hold on to our rapidly diminishing time for relaxation before we had to do the animal rounds again and clinging to feelings of Christmas spirit we had another quick clean up so we could resume the present opening ceremony.

Tia having helped clean the floor of spilled cider was now snoring drunkenly on her bed, Mick replenished the drinks, I slumped on the settee, in the process kicking over my glass of red wine, spraying it everywhere, off we went again. Well, if all bad things go in threes we should be guaranteed a good time from now on, helped along by the growing stock of homemade wine in the pantry we made sure the day ended on a high.

Two days later the weather had changed again and although cold, was dry, with no wind and the sun was out. Mick's thoughts turned to making the big garage/store watertight, a two-person job. So despite it being my birthday I pulled on five layers of clothing, 3 pairs of socks, woolly hat and thermal gloves before joining him. Leaving behind all thoughts of past birthdays spent in pyjamas on the settee armed with a box of chocolates, glass of Baileys and DVDs of Oliver, Paint your wagon and Grease, my one day of total 'me time'.

Hey ho, there I was, 14ft up balancing on the exposed rafters trying to ensure the three metre long insulated corrugated steel roof panels Mick lifted up through them were balanced on the top of the outside wall where I held them before he joined the rafter balancing act to try and manhandle them into place on the pitched roof trusses. The thick panels were really heavy and unwieldy; balance was key to not dropping the things and doing us, or the building, damage in the process. Lacking the necessary lifting kit and necessity being the mother of an invention, an ingenious use of a tow rope saw us roping the panels at the end which was to go on the eaves and continue the rope up the middle of the panel to loop it over the centre beam with me holding the hanging end to ensure the panel couldn't drop whilst Mick juggled it in place, before it was heaved and joined to its predecessor, blooming hard work but it worked very well. The views over the top of the eaves across the campsite below and over our cottage to the paddock and hills beyond were amazing and kept my mind off thoughts of falling or dropping anything on any walkers, unaware of the aerial acrobatics above the lane.

There were fourteen panels in all, seven for each side and we set ourselves the target of four a day. We were two in when Sue came along the lane, spotting me perched aloft rope in hand she burst into a chorus of Happy Birthday to me and seeing I was trapped aloft, mid panel swing, she kindly left card and pressies at my door, something to look forward to later. As we continued to panel number three the chickens sounded off in the paddock, I thought they were probably just announcing an egg arrival but from his higher viewpoint on the roof ridge Mick shouted 'Fox!' and in a flash all but jumped down and was off to the rescue as I frantically tried to tie off the panel so it wouldn't fall. I raced after him expecting to see blood and feathers everywhere. When I arrived at the paddock fence I could see Mick in the far top corner with Tia and halfway down a circle of sheep and pigs with two chickens in the middle. It was like a scene in an old Western film, the troops had formed a circle to protect the defenceless and repel the invader until the cavalry arrived. Heart racing I found three more chucks in the hen house and one under the old caravan we used as a feed store, all accounted for!! Mick came back still gasping for breath and told me that from the garage he saw the fox chase two chickens down the paddock slope, whether by luck or intention by the time he arrived the chucks were in the middle of a sheep and pig circle which stopped the fox in its tracks. Mick and Tia arriving was the final straw and cheated of a meal the fox was off up the slope and through the fence to chance his arm somewhere else.

Tia's role as guard dog was in dispute as when arriving in the paddock instead of making for the intruder and seeing it off she ran off and brought back a stick for Mick to throw, only realising there was a fox about when Mick was examining the fence the fox disappeared through and she finally got the scent. Fox scent is the doggy equivalent of Chanel and instinct demands it should be rolled all over, so not only did she fail to help protect the stock she also now stank to high heaven. We left her in the garden hoping the smell would die down whilst I put the chickens away with lots of TLC and corn for a treat. We decided to call a halt on the other work so we could give Tia a bath so she could be allowed back in polite company.

Our first New Year as smallholders

New Years eve saw us in reflective mode, raising more than one glass to celebrate that the decision to change our lives so drastically seemed to be the right one. We had spent so long rushing through life spurred on by pressures to conform that having taken the first steps towards 'dropping out', although daunting were proving exciting and so fulfilling that we felt as though we were coming back to living life to the full, rather than going through the motions. The results so far were promising; back to basics was working for us. As we were still in set up mode we decided another year would tell, everything was in place for the self-sufficiency plan to be achieved in 2009. Welsh weather permitting would see completion of all the outbuildings, happy animals, happy humans, a full freezer of home produced meat and pantry filled with homegrown vegetables, homemade wine and preserves.

For now though, back to reality, the fire was dying, we needed to cut some more logs to the right size, check on the animals despite the torrential rain, scary winds, thunder getting too close for comfort, and the icing on the cake, a power cut. After a cold frantic hour and complete drenching later in complete contrast having had hot baths by candlelight; relaxing in the glow of the fire again we raised another toast to life in the valley and contentedly dozed off. What a wonderful way to see in the New Year.

We started the year up at the crack of dawn to take the little boars on their final journey, leaving at 6a.m to be sure of getting there early and avoiding any delays. The forecast was right and we faced black ice and freezing fog, the journey from hell. Well Mick faced it, I spent the whole trip with my eyes closed, silently saying my prayers. Totally OTT but it worked for me and we arrived without incident at Tregaron abattoir and no one in front of us. Paperwork was handed over, in triplicate, yet more forms had to completed before unloading, one a food chain form and the other a commitment to clean out the trailer on return home. The lairage pens already held two large boars and five porkers slightly smaller than ours, all busy exploring and playing around. Our boys bounced out of the trailer, glad to be out, and trotted into their pen, a final slap on the bum from Mick and they got busy making friends through the fence with the others.

We were proud of how well they looked and how confident they were, knowing the good life they had lived would be repaid by the excellent meat they would produce. Some were quick to suggest we were cruel to have our animals killed, whilst buying their anonymous pre packed meat bought with no knowledge or thought of where or how the animals had been born, raised, treated and dispatched, where's the moral high ground in that? Easier not to bite (pardon the pun) and accept everyone makes his or her own choices, we were more than happy with ours.

Returning home we tucked into a hearty breakfast before starting the day jobs, Mick on the animal rounds and me in front of the computer. By lunchtime I was in need of exercise and Mick collared me to help him get the final five garage roof panels in place. He had been lent a small forklift to cap the ridge and by the end of the day I had added forklift driver to my CV. My job was to position the forklift along the wall and then get the ridge capping sections to pass to Mick, simple, you would think? The latter involved moving a number of 6 ft lengths of bendy metal out of the garage where it nestled against our beloved camper, without scratching the sides. Then I had to carry each piece 20ft up a ladder leant against the forklift platform, maneuvering myself and the ridge sections onto the forklift platform and finally sliding the section up the roof, to be grabbed by Mick and put in place. My first attempt saw the ridge section curling over my head and sliding back down the ladder, the second attempt I made it onto the platform but managed to kick the section off the other side, third time lucky and despite almost knocking Mick off his perch the section was finally in place. Only four to go! Pausing to get my breath back atop the forklift I looked at the amazing view around the valley, snow topped hills on one side, sun highlighting the amazing different colours of the fields and forest on the other. I wondered how many other office workers spent their lunch break in similar fashion.

A pleasant end to the month was Les the butcher phoning to find out how we wanted our pork butchered. Building on our previous experience we decided one pig would provide joints and chops and everything else together with the whole of the other pig would go for sausages. The sausages were so highly rated by everyone who had them last time round that we decided to stick with 50% plain but experiment with the other half split between leek, cider and chilli.

If all went well we would repeat the exercise again when the gilts went. We were now able to estimate that two pigs a year would supply all our own pork requirements and anything else would be sold to try and cover costs.

Collecting the following week Les said he would be happy to buy from us in the future if we had a surplus. This would save us butchering costs, freezer space and finding customers piecemeal, a good arrangement if he held to it. As we left Les said, 'whatever you are doing keep doing it!' knowing a butcher rated what was being produced from our efforts was just what we needed to hear, all the hard work had paid off.

Laden with boxes of pork our first job after scrubbing up was to weigh and label, another lesson learned from last time. No more continual dives into the freezer, guessing the weight of the unlabelled joints. Mick's patience wore thin though trying to balance the larger joints in the bowl of my traditional brass scales and cursed having to keep juggling the different weights. We resolved that before we collected the sausages we would buy a better-suited flat bed electronic scale. Despite having the wrong tools for the job the worktops slowly filled with joints and chops weighing in at a grand total of one hundred and thirty two pounds. Fillet, loin, shoulder and leg joints varying from two to five pounds in weight, all meat with just the right amount of fat scored to produce succulent crackling, no stringy bits in sight. The chops looked just as tasty, bagged in fours, more than enough for a family meal. Half the freezer filled, the following week we picked up one hundred pounds of sausages in four enormous bags, one for each flavour, ready for packaging and filling the freezer to the top.

Armed with new scales, rolls of bags and a marker pen to label the types we set up the now familiar conveyor belt across the kitchen. The mix of smells, pork, leek, cider and chilli were mouthwatering and before we started a selection of each were put into the range for supper later. Tia took up position on her bed by the range, head raised, sniffing in anticipation and keeping an eye cocked for anything that might come her way. Two hours later we had four large piles of neatly packaged and labeled sausages. Finally, freezer loaded, all kitchen surfaces and us thoroughly washed, we tucked into our sausage feast, and so hungry we cleared the lot.

Exhausted, I was looking forward to a sound nights sleep and long lie in but at 2a.m was up with rampant indigestion due to the (pardon the pun) pig out so late in the evening and so spent the early hours downstairs pacing the floor and drinking copious amounts of water to dispel the pain. At one point I swore to be a vegetarian if only the pain would go away. The thought soon passed, as did the indigestion!

Keeping warm and snow, snow and more snow

By midwinter the constant efforts to keep three wood fires going was really beginning to hit us. First job of the morning was to get the range going properly, coaxing life back into the embers so that it fired up enough for the water to be hot and for me to cook. The cleaning out the ashes from the two wood burners before collecting more fallen wood from around the holding to be chopped and stored in the woodshed, before cutting the dwindling pile into three log sizes to suit the three fires. Supplies indoors the two log burners were then lit, then throughout the day we had to keep them and the range going until finally at bedtime they were fully stocked to try and keep them in overnight. Due to the variety of wood and burning times it was a lottery as to when more logs would be needed so we had a good excuse for staying close to home. It seemed we were on a continual circuit from woodshed to burner, to range, to burner and back again, and again.

The resulting warm house, rosy glow of the fires and knowledge that our heating bills were zero £ wise was enough to keep us going, especially when oil had tripled in price over the last three years. Getting the oven hot at the right time using wood was proving difficult so we invested in a small electric combi microwave/oven/grill. I took it as a personal failure if I needed to use it but found it reassuring to know that we had a plan B should the range fail us. The range fire dying at night meant we no longer had the continual sauna conditions upstairs at night so at bedtime it was a race to get undressed and into bed before the extremities froze. That wonderful feeling of warmth huddled under the covers whilst the temperature dropped outside was great, especially if you had possession of the hot water bottle.

Getting used to the cold mornings was more of a pain, dithering over what to wear was not an option, too blooming cold. Clothes were piled in order of putting on in the bathroom before bedtime. In the morning Tia set off the alarm, cold nose under the duvet, much more effective than any gadget as you couldn't put her on 'snooze' or you got up to a smelly mess to clean up. Within two days I was managing to be up, dressed and out with Tia in ten minutes, already warm from the effort. Striding out along the lanes kept me warm and on my return Mick had completed fire duties and the house slowly started to warm up whilst he went out to do the outdoor morning chores, breaking ice on troughs and seeing to the animals. As it became colder fire stoking was taking over our days and trying to fit in all the other jobs was nigh impossible. Even with my limited assistance and despite the reduced fuel costs we knew we couldn't keep the routine up for much longer.

Mick checked oil prices and they had fallen considerably since our last fill so we were easily convinced that now would be a good time to change the range back to run on oil again. Whilst we missed the smell of the wood smoke in the kitchen, we definitely did not miss the continual layer of ash that reappeared over everything as quickly as I cleaned it off. The woodpile would last a lot longer and as we now knew that we could live without the range during the summer months our oil bill should be a lot less. Our days were less hectic and lighting the log fires in the evening became fun again rather than a chore.

Big and Little Pig had not come in season, which proved Boris had obviously done his job and as they were both 'in pig' it was time for the two gilts kept in reserve to get ready too go. Following our now tried and tested routine they were relocated to the paddock and trailer bedsit. A luxurious straw nest was plumped up and added to by room service (Mick) every day. Big Pig felt it her right as head girl to take over the trailer whenever she was let onto the paddock. This was quite entertaining until the young girls tried staged a sit in as she forced her way in, setting the trailer rocking to loud shrieks as the fight for possession began. Mick stopped play before any damage was done to pigs or trailer by rattling the feed bucket and the dispute was quickly forgotten as they vacated at speed for the chance of an unexpected feed. Mick shut the trailer ramp door to resolve any further conflict, or so we thought.

Later that day ear splitting squeals and loud banging brought us running from our different jobs to the paddock where it sounded as if murder was being done. A final bang and shriek saw one of the gilts flying out of the old sheep ark and the head of Big Pig slowly emerging with a smug smile on her face at having trapped, soundly spanked and evicted the intruder as she now wanted sole possession of the nest at the back, what a bully! The banging was obviously the sound of the poor gilt being bounced against the sides until she found the exit. No wounds or damage seemed evident, other than to her pride, Mick gave her a reassuring scratch and tummy tickle and she was off rooting about, none the worse for the experience but all the wiser, making sure in future she always had an escape route available.

Snow gently falling on Monday quickly turned to blizzard and by the end of Tuesday we had over six inches on the lane and paths and a lot more everywhere else, it was beautiful to look at, all the trees and gates laden, a perfect Christmas card picture, albeit over a month late. Thinking ahead, I got some great pictures to use for next year's cards, another tick for self-sufficiency. The sheep weren't quite so impressed, the only grass visible being that kept thawed by the warmth of their bodies as they lay waiting for the worst of the blizzard and winds to pass over. They made swift work of the small saved patches and were quick to run down for feed as soon as they saw Mick appear with the bucket. Whilst they were keen to be first in line they really didn't like walking on the fresh snow, perhaps because it didn't feel sound underfoot, it made us laugh to see the different ways they dealt with it. Rambo tried to retain his cool image by lifting his hooves as high as possible and slowly high stepping across whilst the girls threw caution to the wind trying leap as far forward as possible, relying on speed preventing their legs going to far into the snow. The mass of white snowballs advancing at speed down the slope to Mick was like watching skittles in reverse, seven balls aiming for one skittle, Mick. Dodging them as they overshot, he put extra feed into the troughs as reward for their effort, and the entertainment value.

The little gilts first encounter with snow brought a sudden halt and squeals of surprise as trotters sunk in and snouts made contact with strange cold white stuff, quickly followed by a madcap game of chase, spinning and grunting with joy at the spray of snow they could kick at each other. Mick left them out until the snow started falling heavily again, they were more than happy to go back having realised that they couldn't root about without hurting their snouts on the frozen ground and as the snow above was up to their bellies, parts they would rather be kept warm were in danger of freezing. Once settled for a doze in the warm of the trailer home Mick loaded the hay basket for the sheep, this couldn't be done when the pigs were about as they not only dislodged the basket hanging on the gate by using it as a scratching post but also yanked all the hay out at once, only eating a little before throwing the rest about and trampling it so that the sheep wouldn't touch it!

After two glorious days of being snowed in we were bored with being couch potatoes and walked up the hill to the shop to stock up on essentials and hear how the weather had affected the roads further down the valley. Gritters had reached Llandovery but the seven-mile stretch up to us had yet to be treated, it didn't look like we would be going anywhere soon. Local schools were all closed so the only traffic up and down the hill were sleds, not just for the kids as they were adapted for loading up with supplies and then sliding home on, excellent fun, especially after having popped into the Royal Oak for a warm both outside and in from fire and spirits!

It was a big surprise the next day when a blooming great lorry made it to the cottage with a delivery of 300 bare rooted hedging plants, which we thought wouldn't be arriving for another two weeks. They needed to be planted within three days but with the snow falling thickly and ground frozen there was no way we were venturing out. The boxes were stored in the garage and fingers crossed for a thawing in the ground before they died a death.

The next morning we woke to a clear blue sky, sunshine, but no thaw, so we decided to leave planting for another day. Going to get the gilts in at the end of the day one would not come. They were normally both shouting to be fed but despite rattling food and her sister tucking in there was no response. This gilt had more important things on her mind, stalking Rambo. She would not leave him alone, rubbing alongside him and poking him to give her attention; clearly she was in heat and had made for the only male in the immediate area, albeit a different species! Rambo seemed amused by the attention, butting her away gently, she mistook this as a sexual overture and now stood motionless, head cocked, ears forward, rump presented, waiting for male contact. Unfortunately it was Mick, intent on getting her in for the night, not in pig. Calling her, whacking her behind, no effect whatsoever, she stood like a statue. Pushing her, snowball thrown at her bum, still no effect she was in a heat induced trance. Perhaps she thought this was foreplay! Disillusionment came in the form of three fluffy snowballs, bang on the snout, rousing her with a jump, a grunt and shake of the head she came to her senses and trotted home to the trailer.

Next day the snow was still very much in evidence but softening so we bit the bullet and retrieved the boxes of hedging plants from the garage and stood them in water for an hour to let the roots come round before we planted, giving time to plan how they would be mixed. 50% of the 300 were blackthorn and hawthorn with the remaining 50% made up of 25 each of Guelder Rose, Elder, Crabapple, Field Maple Dog Rose and Hazel. A true country field hedge, which hopefully in time would provide good wind shield, cover for wildlife and berries and flowers in abundance for the birds and for our wine and jellies. Holding that thought, we looked at the daunting length to be planted, the full length of our boundary between the pig pond area and our neighbour's horse paddock. Close to the stock fence but far enough away for the neighbour's ponies not to think the plants were a tasty takeaway.

Operation hedge began. I was responsible for laying out the plants in order of planting, Mick digging the hole, me putting them in and him backfilling the hole and firming. The ground although soft was run through with stones and old roots making getting a straight drill a challenge, added to which some of the roots on the plants were so large that a combination of spike and hand digging were needed to ease them in securely without damage. Fingers and knees quickly froze from being in the snow, Mick's back was taking a real bashing from the jarring as the spike hit rock, but despite this we were slowly moving along the line. The trick to staying motivated was to face backwards and see what you had done rather than forwards at the amount you had yet to do.

As the day wore on the sun got stronger, so although in snow, we were now down to T shirts, the ponies in the neighbouring paddock came to heckle and eye up which plants they would try and reach later, whilst Tia thought every plant I put down was a stick for her to play with and tried to run off with them. 150 plants later we were halfway along, but losing the light and the use of our backs so decided to call it a day. After a quick supper, hot bath and spraying each others backs with Deep Heat, which was the closest we got to foreplay these days, we were ready for bed by nine o clock and fast asleep by five past.

The good weather continued and so with our planting system now well established we finished planting the whole side and end boundary with the 2-3ft high saplings, many of which were sprouting already. Promising growth of a foot a year we hoped they would pay back our hard work with a bushy natural boundary. Sat in the garden celebrating the finish and the snow thaw it was hard to believe that two days ago we were hiding indoors from a blizzard. No one can accuse Welsh Weather of being dull.

True to form the next day saw snow replaced by continual drizzle. No chance of any outdoor work so I came back from the post office shop laden with a box of overripe oranges, determined to do something productive. On returning indoors a pleasant hour was spent converting the mouldy fruit into yet another bucket of wine juice.

<u>Orange wine recipe</u>
4lb overripe oranges, 3lb sugar, 6 pints boiling water, 1 teaspoon pectic enzyme, 1 campden tablet, 1 teaspoon wine yeast, 1 teaspoon yeast nutrient
Chop orange rind and fruit, excluding any pith and place in plastic bucket, pour over boiling water, add sugar, stir till dissolved, leave to cool. Add crushed campden tablet and pectic enzyme, cover and leave for 24 hours. Add yeast and yeast nutrient, recover and leave for 2 weeks, stirring daily. Strain into demijohn, ferment until clear then bottle.

This wine is really worth waiting a year for, it is very strong and mixing with lemonade makes a great summer drink, or warms the cockles on a cold day when used to make a tasty variation of mulled wine.

Spurred on by using the wine making kit again I emptied the freezer of the remaining raspberry and blackberry crops and added the resulting buckets to the orange. All three sat awaiting yeast addition alongside the Raeburn and the kitchen smelt wonderfully of fruity decadence. All would need transferring into demijohns in the next few weeks so I set to sterilising donated bottles to free up the clearest 3 demijohns of wine already in place atop the Raeburn. The first two, elderberry and quince, had long ceased fermenting and the blackberry definitely looked finished so the siphoning tube in place I set to. 18 beautifully clear bottles of wine later and more than a little tasted in the siphoning process I was feeling very proud and more than a little woozy as I made out the labels. Writing them was not a problem, drunkenly bending to stick them on straight was, but perhaps appropriate for them to be at a tipsy angle, hinting at the enjoyment within.

Storing it was just as much fun, seeing the stock build up and finding bottles I had forgotten I had made, bottles being put aside to taste later and decide if it was worth making any more of it. Though sat on the pantry floor swaying gently amongst a sea of bottles I decided perhaps postponement of any more wine tasting for another day would be best.

Porkers depart and sheep surprise

Valentine's day was spent in the pigsty, who said romance was dead? Big girls having been given the freedom of the paddock for the day, they promptly evicted the gilts from the wallows they had been digging and made them their own. Left in peace we mucked out and set to fitting a gate divide across the open pen so that we would have two separate farrowing areas ready for the big event. Big Pig was definitely showing signs of having more in her tummy than food and we had the added benefit of remembering how her body reacted last time round. The artificial insemination debacle was done the first week in October so that obviously hadn't worked, but Boris definitely had. Little Pig was the unknown, her sides looked as though they were getting the barrel effect and her teats were swelling, but this could just be growth, still another couple of weeks and we would be sure, based on Boris's time with them litters would be due anytime between the last two weeks in February and beginning of April.

The gilts started getting their own back by annoying the big girls who were now too cumbersome to catch them, that and their growing size prompted making appointment for their departure a week later. With much improved weather, not even a frost, it was a good run and on the way it was great to see the number of early lambs in the fields. We reversed straight into the holding area where one of the guys chatted to the girls as he helped them out and they promptly forgot about us. The disruptive force of the porkers now gone we looked forward to a period of relative calm and preparation for our expected new piglets and lambs. No such luck.

Mick called me to the bathroom window where he was overlooking the paddock and pointed out that either we had got our sums wrong or we had very premature lambing as at the top of the paddock. Speckle face could be seen gently licking a little white lamb as it suckled, I rushed out to check all was ok as Mick shouted from his viewing point that there two. Sure enough, as the ewe turned I could see another totally black lamb with white tail tip and star on forehead. Keeping out of her 'fright zone' I stood and watched as our first twin lambs suckled happily from mum who looked distinctly smug and none the worse from the birth. Both lambs were dry and although stumbling as they discovered what their legs were for, were obviously in good health. Little tails were spinning like tops as they suckled, a good sign that the milk was flowing and good. With full bellies they curled up to enjoy a nap whilst mum grazed for a bit before settling down close to them.

Tony our sheep farmer friend arrived to say he and the family would be down in about twenty minutes to inject the flock with their annual jab. Only the lambs would need to be left out, as they couldn't be done until they were over ten days old. I left Mick to try and pen them as I had an emergency dentist appointment having chipped a front tooth. An hour and £100 pounds later I had a new filling, no sign of any permanent damage and a new belief that not all dentists liked to increase your pain, unlike the blood spattered butcher aproned school dentist, who took pleasure in kneeling on your chest drill in hand whilst nurse and mum held you down telling you everything was all right. The fact that the whole lower half of my face remained numb and I had a real trout pout until the next morning was probably indicative of how much medication was needed to keep me quiet.

By the time I got home all the vaccinations had been done, apparently all the other ewes were in their final stages of pregnancy. The older ones were further along than the two birthday ewes and based on production of the twins by Speckles we could expect lambs anytime from now onwards. Comment had been passed on how well fed they all were, not fat, but a caution for us to cut back a bit. Speckles came to the trough to feed that evening and the lambs bleated pathetically at the abandonment before following her down and settling down to watch what went on. Spring had arrived. Fitful nights sleeping began as we cocked an ear for any sounds of lambing problems.

Next morning all was well. The weather was perfect for new life, sun shining on the newly sprouting grass, twin lambs jumping happily around Speckles, other sheep contentedly grazing. Black faced ewe was holding back but showing no signs of labour and came to the trough all ok so Mick let the big pigs out on the paddock for a treat and they enjoyed basking in the sun as we tickled their tummies. Placing our hands along Big Pig's tummy we could feel the piglets kicking away, wonderful. Little Pig was still difficult to judge, very slight movement, but it could be wind. Mick decided to split them up that night so that they could have a couple of weeks getting used to sleeping apart and building their nest ready for the new arrivals. Big Pig due to her size was staying in the original pen with half the outer pen for exercise and Little Pig was having the other half of outer pen for nest and exercise. Mick built two wooden 'creeper' barriers in the corner of each sleeping area for the piglets to use to escape crushing when mum lay down, put in fresh straw to let them make their nests and individual water troughs. The layout looked really good, the gate divide was a great idea, they could see each other and keep in contact but it would keep the little ones separate until they were big enough to play together and then the gate could simply be opened and locked against the wall giving one big exercise space.

Nature's way

At the end of February our church service was in the next valley at Cyngordy and I had just walked to the end of the lane for a lift with Sue when I heard shouts from Mick as he ran up the lane to stop me going. Black ewe was at the top of the paddock with things hanging from her rear end that shouldn't be; we needed to get her in for a close look. Using binoculars from the bottom of the paddock it looked like her water bags, which precede the birth had come out, but she was showing no signs of labour at all, just wandering about, no pawing at the ground or normal signs.

After a while we realised this was something which we couldn't cope with on our own as it looked like she was prolapsing, basically her vagina was expelled and hanging out, something far beyond our simple sheep skills. We phoned Margaret in panic but she didn't answer, obviously doing her own animal rounds so we left a garbled message on her ansaphone. We phoned farmer friend Chris in Oxford for remote advice, he recommended getting her into close confines so that whatever had come out could be cleaned and put back in and restricted from coming out until she went into labour.

First we had to get her into a pen, easier said than done. With hindsight we did everything wrong, trying to isolate her when we should have got all the sheep to mob and run them in together and then in a more confined space split them up. Realising we were causing her stress we let her calm down before trying to do things the right way, using the quad at a distance to slowly move them all into the pen. Rambo was doing a grand job of spinning to face us to protect his girls; fortunately they totally ignored him and ran off into the pen. I manned the gate as Mick got them to circle and come back out, more by luck than judgment poorly ewe was at the back and so gate shut she was ready for a closure check.

Timely support arrived in the form of Margaret and Tony, having picked up our message and come straight over. Using two gates off the hinges we were able to confine the ewe to a small square 'sick bay', which we lined with dry straw. Margaret had the best reputation in our valleys for lamb midwifery and at lambing time she was much in demand when things went wrong. I was dispatched to collect a bowl of sterilised water, soft towels and lubricating jelly while

Mick and Tony restrained the ewe. Margaret then gently cleaned all the insides, which were now outside, tepid water being used to help reduce the swelling and firm things up a bit. If we had used hot water it would have made them really pulpy, in which state it would have been very easier to tear or pierce sensitive membranes. Then came the traumatic part, gravity was needed to assist Margaret getting things back in the right position so whilst she lubricated up Mick and Tony raised the ewe so she was almost doing a handstand, whilst I supported her head and made reassuring noise, she just stared at me in bewilderment. Margaret very gently and deftly maneuvered everything back in and then, the bit that made me cringe, put a couple of stitches across to prevent anything coming out before the lambs were ready. Finishing with a penicillin injection the ewe was laid gently down on the clean bed of straw with water trough in easy reach and left in peace, with us all keeping an eye from a distance until we saw her take a drink and ease back for a well earned rest.

The ewe was carrying twin lambs which we hoped would be born naturally, the important thing was to keep her settled and hope she returned to health ahead of any birthing. We were to keep her in the sick bay and regularly check so that when she went into labour we would remove the stitches allowing the lambs to be born safely. Margaret was to check her in two days to see how things were going.

Whilst Mick scrubbed up I went to cheer myself up by seeing how the pigs were enjoying their new quarters, expecting to see them both waiting for more treats. Instead I found little pig contentedly trying to encourage nine shiny new piglets to suckle, grunting gently to them with a wide smile on her face. It was my turn to shout for Mick and we watched in wonder at how quickly things settled down. These tiny little piglets were only a few hours old but already jostling to choose the teat, which would remain their very own until they were weaned. Climbing over each other to reach the top row or burrowing underneath for the forgotten bottom teats, a few mistakes along the way, sucking furiously at mums tufts of hair or their siblings ears, but quick to realise there was no reward and clamber to the next protuberance until all nine had laid claim to the teat they wanted, sucking gently, their little tails curled tightly showing their joy.

Boris's influence was clear to see, eight were totally Tamworth in appearance, golden ginger coats and perky ears, the ninth, the biggest showed Little Pig's mix with a multicoloured coat of white and black spots with ginger tints. Big Pig watched with pride the end result of her daughter's very successful first farrowing. I could imagine her grunting instructions through the gate and encouraging Little Pig when things got fraught. Nine healthy piglets for a gilt's first farrowing was a cause for happiness and hopefully a sign that all would now go well with the sheep.

An hour later, Prolapse as she was now to be known was up and eating, but showing no signs of labour. Little Pig was also up, snuffling about as her litter slept in one big heap in the corner. While Mick gave her some sloppy food I cleared away the afterbirth, something that I hadn't seen before and having done so would never mistake for a dead piglet, it was massive and filled a carrier bag. Some advise leaving for the mum to eat, something that Big Pig had obviously done before as we never saw anything like this with her first litter with us, but as it was still there and Little Pig was happily munching slop we thought it best to get rid of. I also found one little still born pig, still in its birth sack, which I cleared away together with any soiled straw before putting in fresh as close to the piglets as I could without disturbing them and incurring Little Pig's wrath.

Big Pig still looking enormous had started to nest but didn't look like doing anything anytime soon. We stayed to ensure Little Pig didn't crush any piglets when she lay down but our fears were groundless, she was as good as her mum, gently pushing them out of the way with her snout until she was sure they were all clear then flopping down with the exhaustion of it all.

That night was sleepless again, filled with concerns that Prolapse would get worse in the night or that piglets would be crushed. Neither fears were realised, whilst listless, Prolapse was on her feet drinking and we tried coaxing an appetite with sugar beet, which she did try to eat before settling down again on the straw. It was clear she had dunged so all appeared ok, a lift of the tail confirmed everything was in place. The sheep troughs were the other side of the sick bay so all the girls and Rambo came down and saw the invalid regularly, as she sat nose against the fence.

When checked an hour later Prolapse lifted her head as if to strain then thought better of it. She didn't seem right and on checking she was really dilated and so I bit the bullet and removed the stitches but there seemed to be no water bag so I logged a call with Margaret as I knew if there was any chance of delivering live lambs something had to be done now. Prolapse just lolled listlessly as I gelled up and trying to remember everything Margaret had told me eased my hand in and contacted a lambs head, following it round to check where its front legs were. It should have been in a diving position but one was behind, this would not cause harm but as the ewe was having no contractions it was very difficult to ease the lamb out. It was not moving and almost certainly dead. I think I was feeling it as much as the ewe, gosh it was tight, but out it came, fully formed and ready for life which had all too cruelly ended before it began. I tried forlornly to swing life back to it, straw up nose, vigorous rubbing to no avail, there was nothing there and Mick took it away.

Prolapse was unmoved, lying with no signs of any following lamb or afterbirth. Margaret arrived just as Prolapse gave a half hearted strain, then gave up, concerned that it had been too long between lambs for the second to be alive she gelled up to examine her. Finding another dead lamb in breech it took a lot to help out before giving Prolapse another penicillin injection and bedding her down in a freshly strawed pen. The poor girl looked really sorry for herself, the penicillin injections would be ongoing to dispel any toxins and help the ewe recover. Concerned that she may not make it I arranged work around her so I could be close at hand. Working from home was brilliant for such emergencies allowing time for both with neither suffering, work life balance never seemed so apt.

On the Tuesday Prolapse seemed a little bit brighter and with help managed to get up although was quite understandably delicate when squatting or trying to lie down. I gave her a 'bed bath' removing all nasty traces and drying her gently to prevent any sores, over the top I know but I'm sure she felt better afterwards, I know I would. Mick was now adept at rolling her for me to inject the penicillin into her rump; she didn't seem to mind at all. Thursday was release day and the speed she left the sick bay belied her delicate state, she made her way to the top of the paddock, where she sat down resolutely facing away from us, small wonder after the experience she had had.

Although she distanced herself from the flock for two days (I said to grieve, Mick said I was nuts!), she was grazing well and on the third day she was down with the rest to the troughs and seemed almost back in rude health and happy to have her ears scratched with the rest of them. We would have a hard decision in the Autumn when tupping began again as to whether we could risk putting her through the same thing happening again, but for now we were happy to see her restored to good health, as was Margaret, who admitted afterwards thought Prolapse wasn't going to make it.

The emotional roller coaster that was February had one more shock up its sleeve. Hearing piercing shrieking, and frantic squawking we saw a hawk diving to attack one of our brown warren chickens wandering in the paddock. As Mick ran to the rescue, we thought it was a goner, the hawks speed was scary, but out of their nests in the copse flew three crows, who with cries of vengeance dived down to see off the invading hawk who dared cross their territory. Chicken with wings flapping madly escaped to Mick who carried it to safety whilst an aerial dogfight worthy of RAF aces took place above. The hawk, its reputation as an unrivalled aerial killer severely dented made off across the valley with the crows cawing and doing victory rolls in pursuit. Scrawny brown chicken seemed none the worse for her ordeal, recovering quickly when given a treat of corn.

We confined the chickens to barracks for the next few days to show any would be waiting predators that there was no free meal waiting for them at our smallholding. Bit of a shame as Spring was showing signs of arriving in the valley and all too soon the weather would return to the wet, windy norm, hey ho, such is life!

Whilst the weather was good we set to transplanting unwanted mature trees down in the Crusher to fill in gaps around the paddock to form a better windbreak and added security. The JCB made short work of lifting an enormous conifer whose roots were over 6ft across, trunk over 20ft high, quickly followed by two similar size albeit smaller root silver birches and a couple of hawthorns.

Ready to bring the trees up I was needed on traffic duty to keep the lane clear so that Mick had a clear run up the scary slope from the quarry onto the lane, as once committed to going up it you really did not want to try and stop. The last hesitant tractor driver who had done so when dropping off a trailer in the quarry had slid backwards into the undergrowth and taken out the Crusher gatepost in the process. Mick went for broke, accelerated hard and crested the lane without damage or loss which was really surprising considering the size of the trees bouncing wildly in the bucket. I couldn't see the JCB for waving branches, to anyone not in the know it looked like an attack of the Ents (if you favour Lord of the Rings) or Dunsinane Wood on the move (if your preference is Macbeth). Having put the trees in place Mick used the JCB bucket to quickly dig the holes and within minutes the trees were in place and with copious watering we very quickly had a mature boundary.

It was amazing to see the landscape change so quickly. The Crusher was great for yielding up plants we could use elsewhere, mainly due to years of being used as a garden dump by the locals. If only we had clicked on earlier to recycling what was down there we could have saved a fortune on hedging plants.

Mad March

     The cuckoo was singing like crazy as she flew round deciding whose nest she would grace with her eggs. Dawn chorus was in last night of the prom mode by 5a.m and by 7 we were up and out to start clearing the garden and paddock ready for the busy year it had ahead. Hindsight is a wonderful thing and over two very bad winters trudging with buckets and feed bins from one end of the plot to the other we realized we needed to have all the animals as close as possible to make it easier to look after them. Being snowed in had given lots of time for coming up with a better layout which would see the main pig pen building extended with more concrete hard standings and covered areas to accommodate chickens, feed, straw, trailer and tractor. Part of the covered area would be left open for flexible use as needed for shearing, vaccination etc.

     First job was to kick-start the vegetable growing plan, recovering bits from last year's veg patch to use in the relocated patch, which would be in front of the old chicken shed. The shed would become a potting shed when the chucks were relocated to their new home. We started unearthing all the canes and running boards that the porkers had either buried or destroyed resulting in a cleared patch of dirt ready for leveling and seeding to return it to lawn. Sunny springtime ended abruptly as mid rake, the skies darkened, blackened completely before opening to deliver curtains of rain that came down so fast it hurt.

     A week later and torrential sleet and rain was still lashing down but tree transplanting had to be done while the roots would still take so Mick resigned himself to being wet and soldiered on regardless. In a rare lull between downpours I took a stroll down to the paddock boundary to cheer him on; the newly planted trees were looking good, the weather was ideal for giving them a good start in their new positions, almost worth the rutted mud bath made by the JCB wheels as they were maneuvered into place, and Mick getting webbed feet. I went back to the 'office' automatically doing a chicken count and checking the sky for any sign of hawk, 6 hens around the hen house, two outside the fence but within easy reach for Mick to get in, no sign of danger and all accounted for. Ten minutes later Mick came in saying he had found scrawny brown bird dead, next to the woodpile by the paddock gate, it had been attacked by the hawk, Mick had arrived too late for the chicken this time. This was bad enough but another brown warren was missing. We searched the paddock, gardens, old pond area and lane for hours without success. Walking round all their preferred hiding places and then swapping routes to double check. I think finding her dead would have been better than not knowing if she was hurt or scared stiff somewhere when it was getting dark and the fox and other predators would be after her.

  We were about to give up when Mick reminded me we hadn't fed the other chickens so I went to get the feed from the caravan. I stood quietly looking across the valley and thinking what a beautiful yet raw place it was when I heard a very faint noise from under the caravan, laying flat on my face in the mud peering through the rain I caught a faint movement of dust in the bottom of Tia's old bone hole and keeping still was rewarded with the sight of the missing chuck, almost buried in dirt but still alive. Overjoyed I tried to coax her out of her sanctuary. No way was she moving, convinced she was safe, but we knew otherwise. By now Mick had joined me and we both used our best persuasive skills, corn and then bread to try and move her without success. We finally resorted to using the broom handle to flush her out, then checking she was unharmed and hugging her tightly carried her back to the chicken house, her head jerking from side to side skyward, checking for more attacks. Safely inside she was straight up to the top of the nesting ladder, none the worse for her ordeal, to tell the others her tale.

  The Goshawk, having identified a potential regular afternoon takeaway, started to pay daily afternoon visits, always around two in the afternoon. We had to break the cycle so it would fly off to annoy someone else and so got used to legging it over in the hen house direction as soon as we heard the crows, our early warning system, sounding off. Suffice to say egg production was greatly reduced for the next few weeks, we weren't sure if this was due to the trauma or sulking at being returned to barracks every time the hawk was expected. Having to have cereal for breakfast was our punishment.

  Mid March Mick came back from morning feed to announce Big Pig was proud to announce 5 new arrivals, all doing well. Unfortunately two had died, one stillborn and one crushed but the remaining 5 were healthy and happily suckling. Big Pig had 12 teats so they were spoilt for choice and hopefully all would now survive. I went to have my first viewing, all curled up in a heap, each with different markings, one white with black spots and the others varying degrees of Tamworth gold with either white socks, white necklaces or black spots, a true mix and easy to identify. No sign of any afterbirth, but there wasn't last time round so we assumed she had had a hearty breakfast.

Last litter Big Pig was really chilled out but this time she seemed quite grumpy when Mick tried to get the piglets into the creep area, she was really vocal and taking the hint as she advanced he jumped back out of the pen and harms way. Her black and white spotted piglet was set on exploring the pen perimeter and we were worried that he was a candidate for crushing as he kept disappearing between the straw and the wall. Happily we were proved wrong. Big Pig was so good with him, nudging with her snout she got him back to the others and then gently pushed them aside so they were clear of her bulk so she could lie down and feed them. She had obviously got the hump when we tried to interfere as mother, quite obviously, knew best.

In the neighbouring nursery Little Pig was following her mum's lead and turning into the perfect mum. As she stood contentedly munching an overripe melon, a treat donated by the neighbours, the piglets played a mad game of chase around her, taking shortcuts through her legs and squealing with pleasure as they jumped over each other, taking time out to push their snouts through the dividing gate to make acquaintance with Big Pig now up and happily munching the other half of the melon on the other side of the gate.

Whilst pleased with the new piggy births we hoped the now enormous ewes kept their legs crossed for a bit longer. The 2 ewes expecting twins, Fluffy White who had lost her first lamb last year and Raggy Ann looked ready to drop but the weather was a nightmare, bright blue skies one minute, torrential hail the next. Twin births can be fatal when it is very wet and cold, as the first-born has to hang around awaiting its twin's arrival and without mum's attention can quickly die from hypothermia. Luckily Speckle Face's twin lambs at three weeks old were safely past the vulnerable stage. The two birthday ewes were expecting their first singles later than the other girls so we had no worries about them.

Lambs have no problem with the cold it's being continually wet that can be fatal in the first couple of days. We made sure the compound ark was laid with straw in case so any lambs born in rotten conditions could be brought in with mums for a couple of nights in the dry to give them the best start possible. We didn't want to confine them ahead of lambing, as doing it naturally in the open was so much less stressful for them as it was their natural environment and they could arrange things to suit themselves, rather than us dictating their movements for our convenience. It just meant we spent much more time checking their movements, alert to any imminent signs of birthing from dawn to dusk and even a few nighttime forays with torches when the weather was really awful.

Fed up with the muddy mess around the field gates and trough area Mick let me use two haylage bales we had been donated to cover the worst so that we and more importantly the sheep would have firm ground to stand on going to and fro the troughs, reducing the chance of them getting foot rot from the continual standing on the churned ooze beneath. The horsey girls from down the lane had given Mick the bales as they were damp and rotting so no good for the horses but they thought they might be useful for the pigs bedding. On splitting the bales though it was quickly evident that they wouldn't be any good, the bales were too far-gone, hot and covered in mushroom spawn in places. I rather hoped the spawn would survive and next year free mushrooms would be on the menu. I spent hours teasing the haylage out and layering before treading well in to firm it down. At the end of the day I was really proud and taking over the feed and water it felt good to not be slipping, sliding and sinking with every step. Smelt good as well. The smug feeling lasted for a week as the weather continued to be wet and windy and the haylage slowly disappeared and became part of the muddy mess.

Pig poo and newborns

At the end of March it had been dry and sunny for a week, unheard of in the valley, a week with no rain was a rarity. The sodden ground which had been a mire since last August was now drying well, grass slowly reappearing to claim the quagmire around the gates, although still very soft underfoot. We decided to start the job of making three level concrete aprons on three sides of the pig sty to enable Mick to complete the winter quarters for the pigs and to provide two more separate outdoor runs, one at the side and one at the back. This would greatly reduce the boggy slurry and give the pigs permanent winter outdoor exercise, keeping all muck out of the building. With the sows occupied indoors with their piglets it was an ideal time to get things done. The plan for the next few days was to define and level the areas using the JCB for the donkey work and then to hire a rotavator to get the areas level.

In no time Mick had dug out and scraped as far as possible with the front bucket of the JCB the area at the back and side, sun was shining, major earth being moved by mechanical means rather than with our shovels and bad backs and all was well with the world. The sheep kept checking on how much grass they were losing but kept well clear of the JCB as they munched contentedly from their vantage point on the slope.

Having saved the best to last our attention was turned to the front of the pigpen, which was a really deep foul smelling boggy swamp containing the winter muck heaps. This needed to be emptied before any groundwork could be undertaken. First Mick drove the quad with trailer to within reach of the rear bucket of the JCB and using the bucket reached over the fence to dig into the foul, wet, sticky sludge of the muck heap and swing it over to fill the trailer. First half, excellent results, the trailer was loaded really quickly with little effort, the JCB really proved its worth. Mick moved the heavily laden trailer across to last year's pig area, cleared by them of any vegetation, now simply an uneven dirt paddock which had been divided to be part new grass run and part vegetable patch. The muck needed to be spread on the latter ready for rotavation, and as we had no tipping trailer out came the fork and shovels.

We set to with gusto, or tried to, the stuff was so sticky and heavy the minute you tried to fling it off the shovel its weight wrenched the shovel out of your hand and it flew across the mud always to land handle down in the preceding smelly, sticky pile. There was no easy way out of it, using forks helped make smaller loads, which could be thrown off, but it still wrenched our arms from the sockets. Three trailer loads of wet, stinking, sticky sludge later the pig pen was almost back to dirt level, we were both bent double, mud streaked, stinky as hell and ready to quit. Traditional Crane afternoon tea of cider and crisps at the oak branch deformed picnic bench facing the paddock we surveyed our efforts. We may never smell the same again or even walk upright but you could definitely see where we had been.

To get another drink involved walking past the feed caravan, because of the time of day and seeing our direction the sheep charged down from the top of the paddock calling loudly for their feed and fighting for pole position at the troughs. In the midst of the chaos I noticed a new arrival, a tiny little white and black-patched lamb still covered in birth bits and its little umbilical cord swinging wildly as it unsteadily followed the others. Bleating pitifully it came to rest against the old pig ark, which on contact it kept butting, trying to suckle. The only ewe missing was Raggy Ann, Mick, bad back forgotten, ran up to the top of the paddock which was not visible from the bottom and shouted back that Raggy Anne was busy cleaning a new born lamb, obviously the second twin and poor little lost one had been ignored while mum was busy producing its sibling. I picked up the crying lamb, all wet and slippery, and carried it back to mum, gently putting it in front of her. Raggy promptly started licking it clean and nudging it to her teats, within seconds both new borns were suckling their much needed first meal, their little tails spinning like crazy as they connected with mum's warm milk.

What a perfect end to the day. It was excellent timing by Raggy, the evening was warm and no rain was forecast so the little ones would be in no danger from the elements and we could sleep well tonight, well at least once we had managed to scrub ourselves clean of pig muck and were duly sprayed with Deep Heat.

Freedom and frights for the chucks

Following the hawk attacks we decided to let the chucks out only when we were around to try and protect them from further aerial attacks. Chickens are definitely not the brainless birds they are painted, ours had obviously spent their time inside planning how they would keep safe. Door opened, they entered the run with the military precision of a commando troop on a covert mission. Keeping low they sprinted in single file, zigzagging from cover to cover to the compound fence, with heads bobbing as they scanned the sky they flew over and made straight for the tractor. As soon as all five were safely under they then repeated the operation to the next target, the quad bike, before a final dash to the caravan, which was next to the hedge. Safely under they celebrated the success of their mission with well-earned dust baths. I was pleased to leave them free to forage out of sight of any predatory air attack.

Busy tidying the wood shed whilst waiting for Mick to come back with the rotavator I was joined by three of the chucks scratching for insects before losing interest and going off to scuff through the snowdrops for any treats. Suddenly a crow sounded the alarm in the back garden and I flew over (pardon the pun) to check what was happening. I couldn't believe it, right next to the chicken run a hawk had pinned down our biggest Black Rock and feathers were flying everywhere. As I charged across the hawk took off and the chicken fled into the middle of the biggest holly bush in the hedge where its pal was already in hiding.

I naively thought they would be pleased to come out and let me carry them to safety, but chickens brains only hold their last thought, in this case 'the minute I leave cover I'm dead!' and the more I coaxed the more they settled into the middle of the holly pretending to be invisible. Having tried to coax them with corn and kind words I resorted to trying to reach in and lift them, bad move, only resulting in my hands and arms becoming a max of bleeding scratches and them moving deeper in. I wanted to check the attacked bird for wounds but considering the speed she ran into the hedge and her ability to evade my clutches it was clear that she wasn't mortally wounded, just sporting a totally bald behind which was probably why she was determined to stay sat on it and avoid any further embarrassment. I left them in peace to chill out while I tried to account for the other three. In the chicken house I found, two playing safe and hiding in the nesting boxes, that only left one unaccounted for, our little brown camouflage expert.

On Mick's return I enrolled him in the search and eventually he found her hiding under the bund wall of the oil tank. In contrast to the other pair she was happy to be picked up and taken to the safety of the hen house. We then combined forces to get the other two out of the holly bush. More corn was sufficient to get one out and safely away but the attacked chuck was determined to stay in the hedge and as quick as we dislodged her she ducked back in. The hedge she was hiding in divided the front garden from the rear garden. There was a two foot difference in ground level either side so with Mick one side and me the other we took it in turns to flush her out and depending on which side she emerged either one of us would make a grab for her. This game continued up the whole length of the hedge, her dodging, us diving, her legging it, us chasing, her getting in back in hedge right up until she made a run for the dust bath under the caravan. In an action worthy of slow motion replay we dived together and caught her between us. We all sat in a heap trying to get our breath back, the chuck was definitely a lot fitter than we were and obviously despite the bald bum, none the worse for her ordeal. Chickens all safely away we couldn't help but laugh at the picture we must have made and what my suited and booted colleagues would have made of it.

Musing over and determined to avoid another shower of manure we donned overalls. Mick started rotavating the old veg patch, quickly moving onto the old pig run and around the side and rear of the pigpen. Having the right machine for the job made all the difference. In no time the dirt and slurry was well mixed and as level as it would ever be. I was delegated to dig out the remaining slurry in the front pig compound, which couldn't be reached by mechanical means. It was now safe to walk on without wellies being sucked off, but it was still quite boggy, due to abuse by Big Pig, Little Pig and Boris during the mating season. Hopefully this would no longer happen once we got the concrete aprons down. Looking forward to this being a one off job kept me going as my blisters burst to be replaced by bigger ones as I tried to get to down to dirt level.

The job took me all afternoon but at least by the end Mick

was able to get the rotavator in without it sinking without trace to give the ground a rough going over. The end result was a vast improvement, the end closest to the pen was quite firm but the bottom end definitely needed another week or two of good weather to be able to work it any more. Cleaning the rotavator seemed to take longer than using it, old baler twine wound tight round the blades packed tightly with mud had to be painstakingly cut off and the machine pressure washed to restore it to condition pre use. Bits of mud and jets of water shot in all directions, Tia tried to play catch at first but quickly took cover in the woodshed as it expelled debris with machine gun accuracy. Mick came in sometime later looking like swamp thing, soaking wet and with bits of mud and straw dropping he made straight for a bath. I followed him with dustpan and floor cloth cleaning the muddy trail he left.

The next day the rotavator was loaded onto the van using a couple of scaffolding planks and taken back, Mick returned with copious amounts of grass seed to start the second stage of land recovery. The sun was still shining brightly as he scattered the seed over the old veg patch that was to revert to lawn and the now smaller pig run which would become another pen for finishing lambs, the remainder being scattered around the field gate areas and other bare patches. To flatten the area Mick had to resort to using the quad bike as our garden roller was not up to the job, the handle dropped off in fright when it saw what was required of it, and we had yet to buy one for the tractor. As the quad went back and forth the clouds moved over and with perfect timing just as Mick finished it began to rain, perfect for the newly sown seed. The next few days were sunshine and showers so any further work on the ground was on hold. The remaining sheep due to lamb, fluffy white and the birthday girls seemed also to be on hold, waiting for nicer weather and in no hurry to produce. Raggy Anne's twins were now quite sturdy and so we had no fear for them or the older twins of Speckles.

Fluffy White and the Birthday Girls lamb at last

Bright and early on a sunny April morning I was in the bathroom, following my normal routine, but not the routine practised in bathrooms by normal people. Our bathroom window gave the best view of the paddock from which we used binoculars to check all the sheep were present and correct each day before any ablutions. I noticed Fluffy white was on her own on the top of the paddock slope, the favoured spot for birthing for some unknown reason. She was straining upwards, bleating louder with each strain, babes were definitely on the way, we quickly dressed and went out to see her.

I was so pleased she had waited until morning when we were on hand to help if needed, especially as following her miscarriage last year some farmers had advised us to get rid of her, as she may not be able to go full term. We so wanted her to prove them wrong. Getting to her feet she stared at me with a grim look of determination on her face and bore down harder, I could see two very long black front legs and head of a lamb determined to stay put where it was, but fluffy white had other ideas, taking a quick rest and little walk before giving a final push which caused the lamb to drop onto the ground, still enclosed in its membrane which it was struggling to free itself from.

I wasn't sure if there was another on the way, especially as she didn't go straight to the lamb so I broke the membrane covering the lambs face, cleared its mouth and nose and was rewarded with it taking big gulps of air and renewing its attempts to free itself. I pushed it towards mum who had been stood watching bemusedly until its head reached up for her and she seemed to snap into natural mother mode and begun cleaning off all the mucky stuff, bleating gentle encouragement. Once free of restriction and bleating back it tried time and time again to struggle to its feet but its legs were so out of proportion with the rest of its body that it kept falling over until mum managed to prop it up against her fleece. The next goal was to get to the teat, Fluffy was so wide and low that the lamb was too tall to get under her at first and just kept butting her side or as soon as it tried to bend down it fell onto its knees. Fluffy was keen to help and next time it fell to its knees moved herself over so her teat was positioned just above his head and all the lamb had to do was look up. We were pleased to see the lamb's tail finally wiggling with pleasure as it latched on.

My mum and brother Andy visited a week later and it was great to show them Fluffy White's new lamb, especially as Andy had found her miscarried one the year before. It was a proud moment showing off the lambs and piglets to the family, together with all the changes since they had last visited. They could see how happy we were with our new lifestyle and I know mum was reassured that things were working out for us. The icing on the cake was that the day before they left Birthday Girl One, went into labour and they were able to watch her very quickly deliver a large single white ram lamb with a black face. They bonded well and the lamb suckled quickly, a perfect memory for the folks to leave with.

The next day it was clear that Birthday Girl One was a natural mum and the lamb was feeding well. Two days later we noticed the lamb had a large yellow lump between its tail and bum, which needed to be removed so it could do its business normally. I carried the lamb into the enclosure, bleating loudly for its mum who ran alongside, while Mick got a bucket of warm water and towel. Marigolds on I set to trying to loosen the tennis ball size lump blocking the lambs bum, apparently caused by the ewes milk being so plentiful and rich that the lamb couldn't pass it properly. We tried holding the thought that at least our sheep milk was top quality to offset the gag making smell wafting up as I finally managed to loosen and remove the offending clot. The ewe stood watching anxiously as we cleaned her lamb of all the remaining sticky yellow goo and then gave it a good drying before returning it to her.

The whole process must have lasted only ten minutes but it was clear from the ewe's reaction that she was not happy with the result, after an hour of sniffing the lamb and turning away every time it tried to suckle it was clear we had washed away the lamb's natural smell. Whilst the ewe quickly responded to its bleating and kept close it was obvious that we would have a problem if she didn't let if feed again soon. Both were enticed into the small compound and into a makeshift pen using a field gate and plywood board in the corner against the stock fence. Safely in close contact with a nice hay bed and trough Mick kept the ewe still against the board and raised her hind leg to let the lamb suckle, tail spinning, mission accomplished, we left them in peace to bond again. Mick repeated the assisted feeding regularly and by the beginning of the second day the ewe was standing still and the lamb was suckling on its own again. The reward was to let them out into the compound for another day of observation before rejoining the flock. Another new experience, which we were pleased to have solved on our own, a hopeful sign that we now knew our sheep and how to help them when needed without scaring them silly in the process.

A week later and Birthday Girl Two was keeping her distance, we recognised the signs and knew that within the day we would hopefully have our last addition to the flock. All day she was restless along the top slope, each time she settled down we got hopeful then after a while she would be off and wandering again. At last just before 4pm she started pawing the ground and turning before settling on her chosen birthplace in the same place as Fluffy White at the top of the slope in the far corner. I can understand why they want to be on their own but why they chose the spot closest to the boundary where they know the fox prowls is beyond me.

Within minutes of settling she went into a very quick labour producing a single white, speckle face lamb, the biggest yet. She was quick to clean it and mother it but would not let it suckle. After an hour we brought her in to the pen, this time enticing her with food and carrying the lamb behind her. Mick then rolled her and put the lamb to her teat to which it latched and suckled with gusto. Having repeated this another two times we were pleased to see that by the morning the ewe was happily feeding on demand and so was let into the outer pen where having proved herself an attentive mum she was rewarded by being allowed to go back to the flock to show off her first lamb.

Having now finished our, albeit small, lambing season for the second year we had now experienced miscarriage, prolapse, still borns, rejection and last but not least constipation. We were beginning to understand that books may give you an idea but a hand on experience is the only way to learn. Looking back at how we tried to get the sheep to do what we wanted without knowing how they would react we realised had made things twice as hard for us. Now having learned to work with them things were really coming together.

Weaners to porkers

Now over three months old the piglets had become independent of mum and so were now ready to be weaned. It was time for them to leave their mums in peace and start living on their own as they grew into porkers. As the old pond had almost dried out the mums were to be given a real treat and let loose amongst the bracken and acorns, wallowing in the still boggy bits. A proper thank you for all their hard work with their litters and a chance for a good long holiday before they were ready to date again. Long grass strimmed, the electric fence was put in position and the pond ark bedded with fresh straw. Big and Little Pig needed no encouragement to go over the bank, as soon as the field gates were opened they were off, barking and snorting as they raced to get back to the remembered freedom and delights of the old pond, acorns galore and more boggy wallows than you could shake a stick at. Piggy heaven, they really were happy as the proverbial pigs in muck.

The Coleg had decided to have all of Little Pigs weaners, so their move was next. Happily diverted into the trailer and taken along the track to their new home to be reunited with dad, Boris, albeit the other side of the fence with a nice overgrown field to play in. Big Pig's weaners remained in the front half of the pigpen; unfazed by mum's vacation they were intent on rooting their own wallow and establishing the pecking order now mum wasn't top of the list. The four boys were obviously developing quicker than their sister but left her in peace whilst they rough and tumbled for pole position.

As spring merged into summer we were alerted to Bluetongue, an awful sheep disease carried by French midges, which had surfaced in the South of England. Whilst midges inundated us in the summer and autumn it was hard to imagine any in French T shirts getting as far as the Welsh valleys. If they did we were sure the Welsh ones would see them off, still, DEFRA advocated all stock were to be injected and we duly collected our allotment together with needles for the job. Another new experience, unlike antibiotic injections which go directly into the muscle and so are a simple stab into the rump, these like Heptovac had to go under the skin but no further. Having seen Tony and Margaret do the deed we felt confident we could cope with Mick holding the sheep still and me injecting.

Having half the pigpen available made the job a lot easier. The back door was left open and sheep food left in there. Prolapse, always first to seek out unexpected food went in and then over the next few days more followed until by the end of the week the whole flock were going in for a mid morning snack. Armed with the Blue Tongue vaccine and needles we used a board to usher them into the feed end for treatment. Rambo first, then the ewes and lambs, with the lambs being ear tagged at the same time. Finally all were vaccinated, including me, in doing the lambs and trying not to put the needle in too deep I somehow managed to push the needle through the pinched skin and into my thumb. Concerned, Mick phoned the vet to check if I would suffer any adverse affects, obviously not, they just told him to watch out for any signs of me on all fours grazing with the rest of the flock!

We then set about separating the lambs and Rambo from the ewes to give the mums a chance to get in tiptop condition before it was tupping time again. There was good grass all around the old pond banks and lots of tasty brambles and saplings so that was to be the ewe's new home for a while, out of sight and sound of the lambs. Using the tried and tested temporary fencing from the pigpen gate to pond gate using a line of electric fence posts hung with bright orange builders plastic, all went to plan. We definitely had the hang of finding the edge of their 'flight' zone and then slowly moving in so that they flocked exactly where we wanted them to go rather than bolting backwards in all directions as happened the first time we tried. Sheep just focus on the clearest run to freedom, so the solution was to narrow the escape routes until the only way forward is the direction you want them to take.

Pride goes before a fall and having got them into the old pond area the plan went quickly downhill. Running over the bank the ewes saw the pigs trough and not having seen an electric fence before Prolapse and Fluffy White picked up speed and in their keenness to get to where they thought food would be ran straight through, pulling the fence poles down and tangling the fencing in the process. Mayhem, the pigs came to repel borders, we tried to lure the sheep out with feed, which promptly brought Big and Little Pig charging over and chasing them off, whilst the other ewes on the outside tried to get in. After a hectic half hour of chasing, cajoling and threatening we finally had the sheep intruders cornered, think Steve McQueen at the fence in The Great Escape. They stared at us, then the fence, then each other and with one accord rushed the fence and jumped over, unlike Steve they were successful and trotted off to join the others who long ago bored with the drama were now happily grazing on the far side of the pond bank.

After mending the fence and feeding the pigs it was Rambo and the lambs turn to relocate. They were to be moved to the run alongside the length of the paddock, which had a gate into the garden at the top end. Being the furthest area away from the pond we hoped it would be less stressful for the newly weaned lambs, totally out of sight and sound of their mums and with a glut of fresh grass. Mick had made another small corrugated iron ark and placed it at the garden end next to a water trough so that they could be easily sheltered, checked, fed and watered from the garden gate. Unlike the ewes the move simply involved catching Rambo's attention with the feed bucket and running hell for leather for the bottom gate from the paddock to the run, Rambo and the lambs in hot pursuit for the bucket contents. Safely in, gate closed, feed dispensed and all happily feeding it was finally our turn and we went for a much delayed, but well earned cooked breakfast, after which, like the animals we were in need of a rest.

Rambo seemed to enjoy his new parenting role, first showing them that it was best to let him have first choice of bed space and titbits or face the consequences. Even though five of the seven were ram lambs their little horn buds and attitude were no match for dad's. He rewarded them by showing how horns weren't just for fighting and could be used to good effect to get them all treats. We found out how when we solved the mystery of why the first two tall poplar saplings lining the run were leafless. The lambs were jumping at a poplar, alerting Rambo to the tasty leaves above, he then slowly butted the sapling low down so that it slid round the spiral of one horn until it was trapped in the middle. Then the clever bit, he slowly walked forward, which bent the sapling parallel to the ground and within chomping distance. As the tastiest bits were at the far end the lambs set to with gusto ast Rambo couldn't charge them away as the sapling would get free and everyone would lose out so he contented himself with steadily advancing, munching away as quickly as he could. As the line of poplars stretched the length of the run the system was quickly perfected and within the week they had cleared the lot of any foliage, but left the sapling intact to produce more for them next year. Teambuilding exercises are obviously not restricted to humans. If we were to get any proper growth from the trees and hedging both there and around the pond we would need to fence them off from the sheep but it was much too big and expensive a job to do for now so we resigned ourselves to checked growth at least once a year until we could get it done.

The ever-present showers joined together for almost the whole of July, turning piggy pond paradise into a water park. Three times Mick had relocated the ark to dry ground, but now it was time to call it quits. More paddy field than pasture the big girls were in danger of developing webbed feet and it was obviously no fun for them not being able to root round. Big Pig's litter were now more porkers than weaners and would be leaving us in a month so it made sense to move the big girls back into the empty half of the pig pen and let them all share the paddock when it was dry enough for them to have a run. Electric fence turned off; we thought a simple rattle of feed would see the girls off like a shot, wrong as usual. They remembered the shock the fence could give them and were not keen to repeat the experience. No cajoling could get them to step over it, in the end we had to remove all the posts and wire before they would come through. Safely on the other side they were glad to escape the waterlogged area for the warm and dry freshly strawed nest in the pigpen, catching up with the porkers through the dividing gate.

My raspberry canes had produced nothing this year, never having recovered from the lambs' forays into the garden. Though I still had raspberry wine in the pantry I was bereft of jelly and so I resorted trying to find late wild raspberries in the hedges around the garden. I only needed a pound or so to make a few jars. Finally ripe for picking I made for the hedge with a bowl, quickly joined by two of the chickens; scavenging for anything tasty I might drop or throw them. The team advanced along the hedge, me on my knees in the lead, them diving for any rotten berries I dropped for them, they loved them, unfortunately so much so that instead of following me they went in front and started jumping up to peck off any raspberries in reach, cheeky beggars! I knew how Rambo felt trying to beat the lambs to tasty bits; it became a race for me to get all the raspberries before the chickens bouncing up and down in front of me. Their antics made me laugh so much that I didn't have the heart to put them in and as a result ended up with only a pound and a half of fruit for the freezer, plus two exhausted but happy chickens who had to be lifted back into their run at the end of the day. Practical as ever Mick questioned why I hadn't simply given them some bread in the top garden to keep them occupied, what and miss the entertainment?

After six weeks of constant rain we celebrated it reducing to regular showers, a proper Welsh summer. Hay harvest had been ruined for many, though the majority wise to the unique weather in the valley settled for early silage instead. Pigs are more than happy to sleep in when the weather is wet but now relished the chance for a run whilst it was dry, the big girls happy to mooch about, the porkers going crazy at the chance to have unconfined games of chase around the paddock. We wasted a lot of time watching their antics as they criss crossed the slope at speed, rushing through the bracken patches and in and out of the ark.

The boys were definitely maturing, playing piggy back with each other, with no idea what they were doing it for. Things got a bit more serious when we noticed them turn their attention to Little Pig, who promptly saw them off. Now at six months old they were definitely ready to go and we didn't want to delay much longer in case they started causing problems with rising sexual tensions in the camp. Luckily the gilt would not mature for another couple of months so she was not a target for their attentions.

Dates agreed we let them enjoy their final week of freedom. It was difficult not to laugh at their attempts to woo Little Pig, she was bemused by the attention, the four suitors added together would make one decent boar. The day before they left I spent best part of the afternoon shooing them away from her, despite her running straight after them and waving her rear in their direction, temptress. The final straw came when trying to get them in, Big Pig and the porker gilt went straight in, turning round I saw Little Pig, big smile on her face with all four porkers piggy backing her on all sides. Chasing them off and giving her a slap they were all confined to barracks until loading time.

The hedgerow in the field behind ours was lined with blackberry bushes and as I walked Tia there every morning I kept note of how they were coming on with the intention of having one big pick, but because dry days were few and far between no sooner had some ripened then the rain took all their taste away. A quick change of plan and I started taking a bowl with me every morning, freezing the smaller amounts on my return home in the hope that I would get enough to make into enough bramble jelly and wine to last until next year. The plan worked well, picking in short bursts meant my back didn't suffer unduly, nor were my fingers stained beyond recognition and Tia didn't get too bored. After a fortnight and supplemented by those I found in the garden and pond hedge I had over ten pounds of beautiful blackberries in the freezer, result!!

Hardstandings and hounds

It had not rained for three days so we went for broke to try and get the pigpen concrete hard standings finished before the weather turned against us again. JCB was brought up from the crusher and to make the best use of the weather and working time the excavations and the remaining slurry was taken across the paddock and used to cover all the damage the pigs had done to the paddock boundary posts and fencing, filling exposed gaps and making it more secure. It seemed ironic that what they produced as a result of foraging under the fence was being used to remedy the problem, what goes round comes around I guess.

I was gainfully employed, armed with shovel and rake, directing Mick to dump loads as close to the fence as possible, without wrecking the fence with the JCB bucket, then trying to even out the dumped load along the length of the fence. I had a team of chickens to help, raking the fresh dirt for titbits. Tia was on constant circuits, supervising chucks, then following the JCB from one side of the field to the other. By the end of the day we were dead on our feet and had trouble standing upright but had two areas ready for surfacing and a repaired boundary bank, no pain no gain. Mick reckoned two more dry days would see the job completed, which was a big ask for Welsh valley weather, I said an extra prayer that night.

Fate favours the brave, or is that foolish? It stayed dry and bright and as soon as we'd prepped with liberal applications of Deep Heat we eased our already aching backs into work mode. First the JCB had to be got off the paddock and taken along to the top of the lane to the scalpings pile, some of which would form the bases for the hard standings. Then Mick had to hitch the tractor to the 3 tonne trailer in The Crusher and bring it up to be loaded with scalpings by the JCB, before bringing both back down the lane and into position in the paddock to unload where needed. I was gate opener and lookout to keep the vehicles clear of fence posts, or dog walkers. To keep up I had to run from one field gate to the next, making sure the sheep stayed put, chasing off Rambo who was convinced I had food and shutting gates again as soon as Mick was clear. An hour later and Mick dropped the first load of scalpings for me to spread, another hour and he had them tamped down, ready for concrete. We were on a roll; the sun was still shining and so decided to go for concreting at least one hard standing before the day was out.

Setting up the mixer and things needed was a pain as we had to get across the dirt part of the pen, which was still boggy mud. A quick scavenger hunt around the plot to find as many pallets and scaffold boards as we could let us lay a makeshift working platform for the concrete mixer to go on, a run in for the barrow, space for sand buckets and a dustbin to fill with water for the mix. I ran the electric cable from the house; some 60ft or so, making sure all the plug extensions were wrapped in bin bags in case the weather turned, then the hose pipe from the outside tap into the bin. Finally Mick brought round the little wooden trailer loaded with cement and sand bags and we were ready to start the job.

Mixer spinning, Mick shovelled in scalpings from the trailer whilst I collected buckets of sand and water for him to add to the mix, together with the cement. Armed with rake I assumed position in the base ready to spread the resulting load he delivered, precariously balancing on the running boards before tipping it over the timber frame. Eight mixes and four hours later it was done, we had lost the light and could hardly see but we were so exhausted we really didn't care. On automatic pilot we washed off the mixer and tools before trying to wash ourselves of all the spattered concrete, now set hard on skin and in hair. Hot baths and hot toddies in front of the fire an hour later we celebrated our 50% success, one down one to go, weather and backs permitting!

An all too short but blessedly uninterrupted night saw us up bright and early and almost upright. The first hardstanding was set well, sun was shining and inspired by thoughts of solid ground to walk on in the coming wet season we cracked on with getting the back one finished. All was going well, I was managing to keep up with Mick and spreading the concrete before it went off when suddenly everything kicked off. Demonic baying and howling heralded hunt hounds suddenly leaping into the paddock and running round in all directions. Having got over the shock Mick took off trying to chase them out whilst I caught Tia and shut her in the store at the back of the sty whilst I joined the chase off, concerned for the wandering chickens and lambs, as well as any unwanted footprints across our wet concrete.

The hounds were obviously out with the hunt, but there was

no sign of horses or humans. Having completely lost the scent and without any instructions they were wandering round aimlessly. As fast as Mick chased them out into the lane more of the pack appeared from down in the Crusher, leaping the fences and confusing each other even more. As fast as the riot started they suddenly took off, must have been a call beyond our hearing, sudden silence and two mad people stood with rakes and shovel aloft left wondering if they had imagined it all. Light relief over we returned to let out a sulking Tia and spread the abandoned mix before the concrete went off, mending the fences damaged by the hounds would have to wait. By the end of the day we had achieved the objective, both hard standings completed before winter with no money spent on outside labour.

The weather had really worked in our favour as the next day it started raining again, which other than feeding stock gave us a well-deserved day indoors with nothing more strenuous than watching TV to tire us and muse on all the jobs that were being completed. The money we saved by Mick doing everything, building, electrics, plumbing, oil servicing and mechanical repairs to name but a few was effectively his wage and when we worked out how much it would cost to pay someone else to do all the jobs we realised he was 'earning' a lot more than he did when in full time employment. Adding to that the pleasure of working for our future together rather than someone else it made us feel opting for self-sufficiency really was beginning to pay off.

Dagging the lambs

The good grass had been excellent for fattening the lambs that were now very much ready to fill the freezer for another year, but the rich feed was proving dodgy the other end, resulting in the fleece around their rears getting clogged with yukky solid bits that really needed attention. At the moment all it was doing was making them musical, the hard hanging dreadlocks banging together as they walked. We wanted to make sure they were comfortable for their remaining time with us and in good condition to present to Tregaron so sought advice from Tony on what to do, "Dag them," he advised. Dagging the lambs sounded like something you could get locked up for but on further explanation simply meant cutting the clogged fleece away. The term 'simply' by no stretch of the imagination should be used to describe what in my mind was the worst animal job we had had to do yet.

Lambs duly corralled at the end of the day before feeding we decided to dag and worm each one to help prevent any further problems. The wormer was an oral mix, which we prepped ready to give once the other end had been dealt with. Using syringes without the needles was just right for getting the drench into their mouths and over the tongue to make sure it was effective. The dagging shears were fearsome to look at, like a medieval torture instrument, metal tongs with large fiercely sharp triangular blades, the object being to hold them in one hand, closing to cut then relaxing to release the debris.

Duly armed, Mick held the first victim fast, at which stage I belatedly realised yet again I had drawn the short straw and would be at the rotten end. As I got to grips with holding the shears and the offending lumps of fleece I mentally added a gas mask to the list of kit for next time. Hands deep in the disgusting nether regions it took until lamb 3 for me to get the hang of the shears, quickly and cleanly cutting the offending lumps, rather than my earlier hacking and sawing. Despite my inexperience making it a long job the lambs seemed to appreciate my efforts, standing still between Mick's legs, chewing cud quite oblivious to the hell I was going through.

As dusk fell another failure in preparation was evident, no midge defence. They didn't bother the lambs but were intent on biting any bit of us they could get to, as I hadn't firmly tucked my jumper into my jeans the exposed strip of flesh on my back became a smorgasbord for them and the pain of the bites was intense as I tried to finish the last lamb off. Job done, mess cleared up and dark descending we heading indoors. Spattered in questionable substances we stripped off in the utility room and put everything we had on straight in the wash before running for the bath and shower.

I made the mistake of having a hot shower, which activated the itch factor of the midge bites, it was hell, but at least I no longer smelt of the contents of a sheep's bum. By the morning I was in agony, all the bites had swollen to mump size and anything against my back caused them to irritate even more. This time Mick drew the short straw and had to regularly coat me in various potions. Three days later assisted by two packets of antihistamine tablets, two tubes of itch relief and a bottle of calomine lotion, I felt better, and had learnt to my cost overalls should always be worn when working outside at dusk. The lambs looked a lot happier, even if a few sported rather strange rear end hairstyles; they must have been the first three I did.

Bonfire night heralded the end of Rambo's time with the juveniles and the beginning of the joys to be found in the red light area of the paddock created by the ewes now in season and keen for male attention. Devilish grin firmly in place he sprinted over to start making his girls happy. New beginnings very much evident it was time for the lambs to depart. The circle of life completed.

As the weather got worse it was good to know the animals were all assured good shelter and ground for the winter. Big and Little Pig were spoilt for choice with their nests in the pigpen and two outdoor runs to choose from. The flock had dibs on two strawed arks in the paddock when they wanted shelter, or a hiding place from Rambo. Life settled into a more gentle routine without the youngsters, no more trying to stop the porkers misbehaving or continually freeing stuck ram lambs whose horns had trapped their heads in the stock fence.

Unexpected early Christmas presents

At the beginning of December the rain and high winds gave way to bright but cold winter days. The range was turned up and the two wood burners were kept in overnight ensuring a warm welcome inside. The pigs had taken to sleeping late, only rousing with a few grunts when we opened the feed bins. On going over this morning I could hear loud squealing as soon as I left the house. Both girls were waiting at the dividing gate for their feed, all looked well, but why the squealing? Turning to their nest I saw seven tiny piglets crawling around squealing for a teat, on cue Little Pig went in and lay down to let them suckle. We didn't even know she was pregnant, not a sign, no clue, a quick mental math's calculation and though it didn't seem possible, that one day of fun and frolics with the boar porkers had obviously done the job. What a wonderful early Christmas present, as I left the pen to get Mick, snow started to gently fall, perfect.

It was a simple matter to lay a nest the other side of the pen and replace the dividing gate, moving Big Pig into her own suite. This would prevent sow conflicts or accidents with the piglets. Though successfully born without any losses it was only fair to give them all as much space as possible. Nests plumped up we spent an hour or so watching the bonding of the new family. Four boys and three girls, six predominantly ginger with odd black markings and one white with black patches, they all looked well formed and had no problem suckling. Nature has a wonderful way of sorting things out, we could now defer a visit from Boris until the New Year to get Big Pig 'in pig', as this unexpected but thoroughly welcome surprise litter would ensure continuous pork for next year. Little Pig was duly rewarded with a smorgasbord of piggy treats, with Big Pig being given her due for her role as midwife.

The gentle snow fall became persistent and by 19th December we were totally snowed in, which was great, no one in, and no one out, all festive stress relieved by circumstances totally beyond our control. No frantic round of visits and endless traffic jams, just nice long phone conversations in front of the fire and promises of catching up in the New Year. Our main social event was trudging through the snow up to the little shop for milk and potatoes before popping next door to the Royal Oak for mulled wine, a warm by the fire and chats with likeminded adventurers.

Another bonus would be the bank balance in the New Year, not being able to shop in the week before Christmas meant a huge saving as it's always amazing how having watched the idyllic TV Christmas commercials how many things I become convinced I cannot do without and normally rush out to buy in a panic, paying over the odds, yet still find the items in the pantry, well past their sell by date in the New Year. Yes, I did miss no brandy butter for my mince pies and my hastily made substitute with brandy essence wasn't the same, but it was fun making do. Fresh veg for Christmas day was looking a bit remote, the contents of the veg rack having dwindled to six potatoes, two oranges, a lemon and a very sad looking parsnip which normally would have gone to the pigs. We did have one pack of our runner beans in the freezer but nothing else as I had been running the pantry store down in prep for a big pre Christmas shop, silly me. At least we could have a bird; diving into the bottom of the freezer I had found a small chicken, which would do the job nicely.

A tip for anyone thinking of living remotely, make sure you live near a council road worker. In previous years the council gritted the road from Llandovery all the way to St Barnabas as one of the council road workers lived in a cottage in the lane opposite ours, and it was essential he could get to work to help clear the roads. Unfortunately for us Tegwyn had now retired and so now all we got was the occasional drop of a pile of grit at the end of the lane for communal use. As this was dropped in the autumn by the time it was needed the piles had either disappeared, got snowed over or was frozen solid and so of little effect. So although the top road from the Post Office to Llandovery would be driveable with care we couldn't get to it safely.

Heavy rainfall raised our hopes for a thaw but the rapidly dropping temperatures meant it froze on top of the remaining snow so the lane became an ice track, ok if you had a bob sleigh but getting up the slope to the top road was definitely not on the cards. Hey ho, Mick resorted to watching model car racing on Men & Motors whilst I decided Christmas wouldn't be Christmas without shortbread and fudge and so dug out a couple of Delia recipes. Whisky fudge was an option and as I had won a cheap bottle of whisky in a raffle but neither of us drank it I thought it might be a good way to use it up. The recipe only used a tablespoonful so the bottle was going to languish in the pantry until when on the phone to mum she told me she had a recipe for a Baileys substitute which was as good as the real thing. I do love a nightcap of Baileys over the festive season and so the unwanted whisky was put to good use resulting in three bottles of extremely tasty Whisky cream liqueur. I actually thought it was better than its Baileys counterpart and at a fraction of the price.

Whisky cream recipe
1 mug of whisky, 1 mug of soft brown sugar (or any sort), 1and a half tins of evaporated milk, 1 dessertspoon of coffee granules - whisk in bowl, bottle and drink!!

Being snowed in was really giving us back our love of Christmas; it was so much more fun to be making all the festive treats and taking time to decorate, gradually building up to Christmas Eve. Pre move years we would have been rushing about until the eleventh hour in a continual round of shopping and visiting, with no time to appreciate the joy of preparation and anticipation let alone any time for each other. Being cut off definitely had its benefits; starting the festive season totally relaxed rather than totally stressed was a welcome early present.

All outside taps were again frozen solid so with a sense of de ja vu we resumed the three times a day trudging to and fro between kitchen and troughs, filling buckets with hot water to thaw the water butts enough to fill the troughs. That together with feeding the pigs, chickens and sheep two times a day and chopping wood and stoking the two wood burners from morning to bedtime made sure we had no time to be full time couch potatoes, but we did our best. In-between rounds flopping gratefully in front of the fire to defrost with a mug of tea and snacks, watching Zulu and other Christmas telly treats yet again before turning out for the next water round. The piglets were now playing happily in the hay nest Mick had made them in the sty, Little Pig was happy to have the other area to wander in for a bit of privacy. Big Pig, the other side of the gate in her own nest had the advantage of getting out on the paddock to steal the sheep food twice a day, though she didn't like walking on snow so was quick enough to come back in once she had cleaned out their trough.

The chickens were content to stay in, they really didn't like the snow and preferred to stay in the nesting boxes, good for laying and thanks to the five extra warren hens Mick had added to the flock we were getting a minimum of seven eggs a day. Unfortunately our neighbours either couldn't get to us to get eggs or were already stocked up and even with our love of anything eggy we were hard put to reduce the increasing number of filled egg boxes taking over a pantry shelf. Mick was starting to eye up the backlog as a treat for the pigs. I love my pigs but I was determined we should get first crack, pardon the pun, at the glut and try my hand at making things which we would normally have bought in.

I spent that evening trawling old cookbooks and scribbled recipes from friends and family to decide the best way to use the most eggs on things we really liked. Next morning still snowed in and with the range up to a decent heat I had no excuse and cracked on, even poorer pun, turning a stack of eggs into a variety of tempting goodies. I decided not to set the bar too high and do it over two days, mainly due to the savouries I had chosen doubling up for both main meals hot and snacks cold. Those not keen on recipes are advised to skip a few pages.

First on the wish list was Lemon Curd as I still had half a dozen lemons in the rack and one batch (three jars) would use six eggs. Made with fresh lemons and butter it was superb, on toast, sandwiching sponge cakes, filling tarts or lemon meringue and even as a guilty pleasure eaten straight from the jar for that instant pleasure hit.

<u>Lemon Curd</u> – makes 3x1lb jars

Juice & rinds 6 lemons (leave out rinds if you don't like 'bits'), 6 eggs, 8oz butter, 1 ¼ lb caster sugar

Put lemon, butter and caster sugar in a heat resistant bowl and heat over a pan of boiling water until all is dissolved and well stirred. In a separate bowl beat the eggs, strain through a sieve into the lemon mixture. Continue to stir over the boiling water until it thickens, be patient!! Heat the jam jars and then pour in the curd. Screw on the lids, tighten fully when cold.

Keeps for a month in the fridge – ours has disappeared well before then!

Next was an obvious choice, Scotch Eggs. We had a freezer full of flavoured sausages so the only other main ingredient I needed was breadcrumbs. Making breadcrumbs is so simple and therapeutic; rubbing three slices of bread in my hands quickly produced enough crumbs to coat 6 eggs. Pure breadcrumbs coat and fry much tastier than the luminous 'Golden Breadcrumb' shop bought drums that contain an awful lot of additives but very little bread. As each pack of sausages had six in it skinning and flattening them into coats for the hard-boiled eggs was really quick and easy.

The pork and leek sausages were first choice for the egg coats and following their success making Scotch Eggs was to become a regular event, experimenting with the chilli and apricot sausages to good effect. If you only have plain sausages mixing them with a couple of tablespoons of sage and onion stuffing mix makes them quite special. Making six at a time served two purposes, providing a good hot meal for two with chips or salad and the other three kept in the fridge to eat as cold snacks during the week. Hard-boiled eggs do not freeze well, they taste rubbery and I wouldn't recommend it.

Scotch Eggs
6 hard boiled eggs shelled, 6 sausages skinned, breadcrumbs to coat in bowl, 1 beaten egg in bowl, couple of tablespoons of seasoned plain flour in a bowl

With floured hands flatten each skinned sausage and wrap it round an egg, pinch edges and roll in hands to make sure the egg is well sealed in. Dip in the flour, then the beaten egg and finally the breadcrumbs. Doing it in bowls means you can roll them round to fully coat at each stage without over handling.

Deep fry in hot oil until golden brown then drain on greaseproof paper. Those you aren't eating hot leave to cool then store in sealed container in fridge where they will keep for a week.

A frittata was next on the list as unlike a quiche no pastry needed to be made and so it took half the time, more importantly it used another 6 eggs. It made an excellent hot evening meal and was just as tasty cold sliced for lunch with pickles and crusty bread the next day.

Cheese & Potato Frittata
6 eggs whisked, 2 medium potatoes peeled, cooked & sliced, 100g cheese cut in chunks & 15g grated for topping, ½ teaspoon mixed herbs (not Rosemary as it overpowers everything – I found out the hard way), ½ teaspoon paprika, 2 tablespoons olive oil.

Heat oil, add cubed cheese, herbs, egg mixture, place potatoes on top, sprinkle grated cheese over, leave on low heat for 15 minutes.

Place under hot grill for 2 minutes – Enjoy!

Having covered the bases with all things savoury I was hankering for something sweet that would satisfy instant snack cravings and use maximum eggs. The easiest and weirdest recipe I found was one in an old village recipe book, 'Impossible Pie'. Despite all the ingredients being mixed together in one bowl before baking on removal from the oven it had magically transformed into an open pie with a pastry base, egg custard filling and coconut topping – impossible, but oh so tasty.

<u>Impossible Pie</u>

Blend together 4 eggs, ½ cup margarine, 1-cup sugar, ½ cup plain flour, ¼ teaspoon salt, ½ teaspoon baking powder, 2 cups milk, 1 cup desiccated coconut, 1-teaspoon vanilla

Pour into a greased 10-inch pie dish and bake for 1 hour at 180°C. Nice in slices hot or cold, with or without cream. Keeps well in the fridge for 3 or 4 days.

Last but not least were a couple of cakes to supplement the Christmas cake and shortbread. Both would be quite happy in a tin or the freezer until needed. Taking advantage of the lemon curd for filling and topping the first a traditional sponge used up another five eggs. This was followed by a complete contrast, an easy Simnel Cake that is much too nice to only make at Easter, a really nicely flavoured fruity spiced cake with marzipan coating which also used five eggs. To be honest it's just as great without the marzipan but making it used yet more eggs.

<u>Vanilla Victoria Sponge with Lemon Curd butter cream</u>

Blend 8oz butter, 8oz caster sugar, 8oz self-raising flour, 2 teaspoons baking powder, 4 eggs, 1-teaspoon vanilla essence.

Divide between two 8inch sponge tins greased & lined with greaseproof paper, bake at 180°C for 20-25 minutes, cool in tins for 2/3 minutes then turn onto rack to cool completely.

For the filling, and if you fancy a topping, beat 4oz butter, 1 teaspoon vanilla, 8 oz icing sugar and 3 tablespoons lemon curd (or jam or leave out) until smooth then fill and top.

<u>Easy Simnel Cake</u>

Sift together 6oz self raising flour, pinch of salt, ½ teaspoon nutmeg, ½ teaspoon ground ginger, 1 teaspoon cinnamon, 1 teaspoon mixed spice.

Cream 6oz butter with 6oz brown sugar until fluffy, beat in 3 eggs then fold in the sifted ingredients and 8oz mixed dried fruit.

Divide the mixture between two 8inch sponge tins greased & lined with greaseproof paper and bake for 45 minutes at 170°C. Cool in tins for 10 minutes then turn onto rack to cool completely

If not using marzipan then slice and put in tin where it will keep happily for a fortnight, or wrap whole in bacofoil and freeze until needed.

Otherwise----

Spread top and sides with jam; I use whatever I have on the pantry shelf, normally blackberry or raspberry.

If you are short of time or eggs buy a packet of golden marzipan and rejoin after the next bit.

<u>Marzipan</u> – 1lb ground almonds, 1lb sifted icing sugar, ½ teaspoon vanilla essence, ½ teaspoon almond essence, 1 tablespoon lemon juice, 2 egg yolks, 1 egg white beaten

Beat almonds and icing sugar together then beat in the vanilla and almond essences, lemon juice and egg yolks until stiff (more icing sugar if too wet and more lemon juice if too dry). Divide mixture in 3. Roll out two to sandwich and top the two cakes. Roll the third into 12 small balls and put round the top of the cake. Glaze the top with the egg white and put cake back in the oven on a baking sheet for 5 minutes at 230°C to glaze the top.

To make it special for Easter decorate the top with little chocolate eggs & dusted icing sugar or if you really like the cake elevate it to Christmas status with royal icing on top and the obligatory miniature Father Christmas.

This keeps really well for over a month, though I'd be surprised if you have it that long.

Total egg count after the cook in? 32, eggsellent! Backlog reduced, the pantry and freezer contents swollen with the results, minus a buffet taster of everything for our supper, home baked heaven.

On Christmas Eve I had one last try at getting a fork into the frozen veg beds and after managing to break through the crust and a lot of wriggling about to not destroy what I was after managed to unearth a harvest of two tennis ball size Swedes, an enormous parsnip that would have won a prize for most obscene shape on That's Life and two handfuls of carrots from ¼ to 2 inches long. To top if off I managed to crack a dozen frozen sprouts off the stem. The harvest may not have been bountiful but it would be enough for us to have a traditional Christmas dinner at least.

It was a magical Christmas day, making do and without all the usual social and commercial pressures. Unlike last year's dramas it was really relaxing and the first time we could remember that we really used the time for what it was intended, a time of reflection and thanksgiving. I would definitely agree that less is more in all respects, the simpler life gets the happier we are.

The lull before the storm

In the lull before New Year and determined to overcome the weather restrictions I decided to do something about being better stocked. Our little shop carried a few essentials but demand often exceeded supply and so it was a seven-mile trip down the valley to the small supermarket in Llandovery, which was a bit restricted and definitely not the cheapest, or thirty miles to Carmarthen to the superstores. More frustrating were the mad dashes for forgotten, necessary items. Ten minutes on the internet resulted in finding that Asda Superstore, although in Merthyr Tydfil over forty miles away, would deliver to the doorstep everything we needed for the grand sum of £3.50.

At worst in the extreme conditions we were suffering we would still get a delivery as far as the shop and Mick could ferry goods down with the quad. As I would save petrol, time, money and my health (no lugging heavy shopping out of trolleys at checkout, back in and then out into the car and out of car at home) and not have to worry about driving conditions I was sold on the idea and spent a happy hour signing up and selecting everything to restock the pantry and other essentials, tins to toilet rolls to cider and everything in between. The resulting bill even with delivery was less than our normal weekly spend yet for four times the goods, hopefully it would go to plan, delivery was to be between 10-12 noon on 30th.

To end the year as it started rain and high winds set in with a vengeance. At least it would help dissolve the snow and not prevent my grocery delivery. I have no problem with rain, cold and snow but winds scare me, as they are so unpredictable. Having lost the chicken house and part of the green house to winds before I was on tenterhooks about what might go next. It sounded so much worse at night because we have no attics and so sleeping next to the pitch of the roof with the wind howling around made sleep impossible, unless you were Mick, who could sleep on a clothesline, he has a great attitude, you can't do anything until the morning anyway so why worry? I wish my mind worked that way. I lay jumping at every bang and crash, convinced the pigsty and garage roofs were being ripped off and the hen house flattened. The morning proved my fears groundless, in fact outside the winds seemed a lot less scary than in.

As the winds continued to batter us I knew I would have another sleepless night but tried to keep it in context and hunted out some earplugs!

The next day the winds and rain kept us in, aided by a well-stocked fire and quality TV (Ninja Warriors and back to back episodes of Lost, still none the wiser!). We roused ourselves for the lunchtime feeding round and saw we had a new feature to the garden, a rapidly rising pond between us and the top garden which gave access to the paddock, caused by the storm water and thawed snow flowing down the valley fields and breaching the top corner of our garden. It was worryingly close to the house so Mick set to with a pickaxe to make a deeper ditch from the breach along the lower garden hedge line to the hay store, which was built over a natural slope to let the water escape down to the lane and carry on its journey across the Crusher to the river Towy below. A job made more difficult due to the overgrown holly bushes in the hedge determined to cause as much harm as possible. As the hay in the store was on pallets the hope was that the water would flow through without damage until a more permanent solution could be found.

Within minutes of finishing the trench it was filled with fast flowing water, the pond much reduced we now had a river running the length of the garden. Soaked through and unable to feel his hands Mick called it a day and made for a hot bath while I strung out coats and everything else on and around the range to dry. Drying things is never a problem if you have a range, an absolute boon not to have to rely on the weather or an expensive tumble dryer to get things dry and aired. The washing machine was always put on in the evening, wet things going straight on and around the range before bedtime and in the morning all is dry, a great timesaver not having to hang things out and be reliant on our unpredictable weather, also the washing smell makes the house smell really nice, despite what Tia may do to the contrary. From the warmth of the front room we watched the fast flowing water, content it was now running in the right direction, away from the cottage, we closed the curtains and settled down for another blustery night.

As promised the next day the Asda van arrived at the gate on time, the driver even followed our online suggestion that as we were single track with no turning spaces reversing down was the easiest option for him. Friendly and fast within ten minutes all bags were indoors and we set to checking the list as we filled all the cupboards, not a thing missing and the refridgerated goods were really fresh and all sell by dates at least a fortnight away. As we sat down to a post Christmas treat, proper brandy butter with the remaining mince pies, we decided we would definitely continue bulk shopping online. It seemed ironic that the traditional grocer's role of visiting rural locations to sell their goods had been restored by the introduction of the Internet.

Rambo and the ewes were reliant on the sheep nuts now as first the snow and now frost was making grazing very poor. They had taken to hanging round the feed trough and shouting if we were late in filling it twice a day. The longest trough was needed to allow for the extra room taken up by Rambo's horns, which he used to good effect to monopolise the food, the trick was to get him positioned at the end so the girls could get a fair share before he started moving round the side where he could dislodge them.

We noticed Birthday Girl One keeping away, after a while she joined the others at the trough but was limping on her front left leg quite badly, although it wasn't affecting her appetite once she had pushed in. Prolapse was also a bit lame on her front leg. Whereas I panic and imagine the worst Mick takes his lead from more experienced shepherds and waits a day to see if attention is needed. Sheep go lame at the drop of a hat and whilst books and internet provide a wealth of diseases which need treatment they neglect to tell you that just as likely is a sprain due to hard ground or Rambo's persistent attentions, hence the pause before action. It's too easy to damage sheep's feet with unwarranted enthusiastic hoof trimming when a simple couple of days rest cures the problem.

Mick set to in the hay store to ensure any further floodwater went under the hay pallets keeping it all dry. Having taken down a redundant compost bin we were able to use the bricks found under it to jack the pallets up, recycling at its best! We hoped our resident feral cat would not be too annoyed at the rearrangement of its bedroom, though we hadn't seen it for a couple of days so it may well have found better lodgings. I made good use of the redundant bin timber planks as running boards across the mud to the pigpen to hopefully spare the ground too much damage from our daily crossings.

In-between outside jobs I prepped a warming winter lamb

meatball casserole to cook slowly in the range, something to look forward to at the end of the day. I had found an old recipe book appropriately titled 'Mighty Mince Cookbook' and was surprised at how limited my use of mince had been until I started using it, the recipes made a welcome change to the previously unchanging Lasagne, Bolognaise and Cottage Pie staples I had stuck to in the past.

That evening as we tucked in our plans for another day of outdoor activity appeared in jeopardy as snow began to fall persistently, lying on the dry ground with the temperature rapidly dropping it seemed unlikely it would be quick to disappear. Our thoughts were with the two lame ewes, we would need to get them in for attention if they were not healed in the morning and really hoped for good weather to do that as we would need to juggle for space in the pig sty to coral the flock, check and treat any feet problems and if treated keep those treated in for an hour or two to let the antibiotic spray take effect.

Cold is one thing we don't have to worry about with the sheep, safely ensconced in their fur coats they are impervious to wet or cold and when in lamb they are kept even warmer. The only thing that can cause a problem is if whilst laid down their fleece freezes to the ground causing them problems getting up, though with the heat of their bodies this isn't something we have yet had experience of. Lambs obviously aren't so resilient, hence our aim to always start lambing during March and April when Spring was well on the way. As normal Mick went to sleep as soon as his head hit the pillow, whilst I fretted over potential sheep feet problems for most of the night.

New Years Eve brought another complete change, running water replaced by a total white out, the sky as white and heavy as the blanket of snow covering everything again. The only colour was a team of 3 bird delegates, robin, blackbird and thrush sent to the front door to get a take out as the snow was stopping them reaching their usual winter stashes and the bird feeders were empty as we were out of nuts. I reduced the remainder of the Christmas cake to crumbs and served them breakfast, trying to stop Tia eating it first and getting her to calm down as she was in manic mode. Tia loves snow; she reverts to puppy, bouncing around trying to pick it up then going skitso shaking it off her snout before rolling over to make doggy snow angels.

Walking the fields was eerily quiet and I was convinced more snow was on the way, though by the time we did the morning feed the sky was becoming bluer and patches of green were showing through the snow. More pleasing was the fact that Birthday Girl One's limp was much reduced and Prolapse was also no worse. As Mick reminded me, Rambo was a great one for being lame one day and fine the next so we took our lead from him and as they were both happily feeding decided to leave them in peace for now.

Mick let the sheep into the garden for a treat, anything green above ground, and they tucked in, only drawing the line at the holly bush. It was great being able to keep tabs on them from the living room window and better entertainment than the telly, especially when they started climbing the fence to eat the hedging along the top. Tia was in her element, cleaning Rambo's horns of snow when he raised his head from snuffling out the grass underneath, with the snow making him a white beard he looked like a devilish Father Christmas.

The river in the garden had slowed to a gently freezing stream and as the sun broke through we decided to let the chickens out for a while as they were going stir crazy having been confined for the last three days. The chucks charged out en masse to scratch and peck at any soft patches they could find and more importantly stretch their wings, jumping the coop and running for freedom across the garden in all directions, it was a joy to watch. No sign of any hawks or smell of foxes so we were happy to leave them out today. There was enough cover under the caravan, picnic tables and hedges for them to get wherever they wanted without fear of aerial attack. The old girls had obviously passed on their experiences the new girls as they didn't hang about in the open, heads down, wings folded for speed they sprinted from one sheltered feeding area to the next. Mick then let Big Pig out, she was pleased to be able to wander around until she realised how cold it was and quickly went back in to warm up. Little Pig and the litter had a good routine now of feed, play, sleep, suckle play sleep, repeated through the day. Little Pig happy now the weather was better that she could have a bit more 'me time' by going outside into the compound.

That afternoon the piglets had visitors, pub landlady Rachel with toddler daughter Daisy, four-year-old friend Sam and his parents. It was great to show them where their pork came from. They were all taken with the antics of the piglets and the big girls, the icing on the cake being the chickens following them across the garden and Rambo and the girls coming to see what the fuss was about. That and sliding on the icy puddles made the children's day, simplest pleasures proven the best. As Rachel was expecting her next baby on 8th January we were concerned she didn't do anything, which would cause it to be an early birth, though she happily climbed a fence to get to the pigsty. We kept our fingers crossed all would be well as although she was thoroughly fed up with the pregnancy and wanted a quick delivery we didn't think our husbandry skills were up to it.

Visiting over and children nicely exhausted Rachel departed to prepare and host a long night of celebrating the end of the old year and beginning of the new up at the pub. We did likewise, armed ourselves with homebrew cider, Baileys and dips (biscuits for Tia!) to celebrate New Years Eve in style, pleasantly content and merry by nine, but despite best efforts were so tired we were in bed by ten thirty. We did rouse to the drifting song of 'Auld Lang Syne' floating down the valley from the Royal Oak and wished each other a happy New Year and thanked God for a very happy old one.

Happy New Year 2010 – back to reality

Beautiful blue skies and warm winter sun gave a promising start to the New Year and we completed the rounds. Big Pig was positively skittish, playing catch with us around the paddock in-between chatting to Little Pig who was taking a welcome break from her litter by sunning herself in the compound outside the pig house. The board Mick had nailed across the bottom of the door was successfully keeping the piglets in, with the exception of one beautiful little golden girl with white face and socks who happily jumped over to explore outside whilst the other six lined up against the board cheering her on, before resuming their frantic game of chase through the hay nest. Having trotted round the boundary under mum's watchful eye, little piglet jumped back in to play with the others.

Piglets have two speeds, madly erratic and static, change between the two is instant. One minute running, rolling and jumping over each other in a blur of excited squealing and the next all fast asleep in a heap in the middle of the nest. As soon as Little Pig came back in it was bedlam again as the piglets fought for teat position even before mum had lain down. We never tired of watching them, but making the most of the good weather we set to trying to clear up the damage done by the last three days high winds and rain, picking up various vessels and empty feed bags blown around the garden, the latter being used to stop up some of the sty windows to reduce the draughts.

The residents of the pigpen were swapped over, Big Pig being confined to the compound and Little Pig and her litter being given the half with freedom of the paddock, only fair to accommodate their growing needs. I went in to prep breakfast while Mick went and collected Big Pig's belated Christmas present from the Coleg, a young boar, descendant of Boris, much more user friendly, no tusks and 3 stone lighter, her own toy boy! Now both the girls had something to keep them happy until the weather improved.

Mid fry up Mick shouting for help rudely interrupted me. Normally it would be a peaceful scene out the front, Tia lying on the doorstep watching the chickens scratching round the hedge, artfully positioned under the branches with the wild bird feeders waiting for the spill as the bluetits and robins pecked bits loose. Not today, the lunatics had taken over the asylum, escaped piglets squealing madly as they criss crossed the garden, spoilt for choice of where to play first, chasing the chickens as they squawked and flapped out of their way, indignant at the unruly rabble disturbing their day. Tia was running in circles trying to round them up but failing miserably as Little Pig thundered down from one end of the top garden keen to find out where her litter were, but taking time out to get stuck into anything tasty in the flowerbeds on the way, whilst Rambo and the ewes appeared from the other end, determined not to miss out on the fun!

It was like watching a speeded up Carry On film, the bedlam was comical to watch but had to be stopped before everything was trashed. Mick set to rattling a feed jug and tempting the errant livestock back to the paddock through the open gate 'someone' had not shut properly after the morning feed round. All was going well, the sheep and Little Pig were quickly through together with two of the piglets; the other five decided it was more fun in the garden and set off to tease Big Pig and Little Boar who were watching bemused from behind the fence in their compound. They caught the piglets playful bug and joined in the fun, grunting and running parallel with them, snorting in frustration when they came to end of their run and the little ones carried on their charge. I manned the paddock gate to let the five through when Mick rounded them but in the meantime keeping Little Pig the other side as an incentive for the escapees to join her. After ten minutes of diving after them Mick was knackered, the piglets high pitched squealing incensed Little Pig enough to push me and the gate aside to get them for herself. Mick, realising she was helping rather than hindering opened the other gate to the paddock so as mum ran back through the garden, calling for her brood they fell in line behind and ran on straight on through the second gate back onto the paddock, finally reuniting the whole litter. All gates secure, animals safe a semblance of order was restored. Who had left the paddock gate open? No name no pack drill! Chickens happily resumed their position under the wild bird feeders and taking their lead we went in for a very late breakfast, now almost lunch, determined to enjoy the rest of the holiday.

Within minutes a loud metal banging and crashing accompanied by high pitched shrieking and raucous crow cries sent us out the door again this time to rescue the chickens, the bloody hawk had returned. As we charged across the lawn we could see the crows chasing off the killer over the gate from the bottom of the garden to the paddock. Suddenly all was deathly quiet, like Sherlock Holmes arriving after the event. We checked the chicken hut, only one chuck in there.

The sheep were all gathered round the gate giving nothing away. From our previous experience with hawk attacks we remembered that when scared chickens head for the smallest covered space where they try to make themselves invisible by flattening themselves to the ground and not making a sound. So I wasn't surprised when despite my rattling of seed and gentle calls of encouragement there were no takers. A trail of feathers from the picnic bench to the hedgerow bore closer inspection and lying down in the muddy grass next to the thickest part Mick could see two chucks dug into the prickliest holly bush. He dislodged one and I cradled her back to the hut reassuring her that all was well and that I would protect her, the look I got suggested it was a bit late for that!

The other one was determined to stay put so we continued our circuit of the perimeters, listening for any tell tale clucks. Despite a pile of feathers by the old caravan and me crawling underneath there was no sign of life, or more importantly death to be found. The only other feathers were by the paddock gate. I stood for what seemed like ages and heard a faint cry which turned out to be a chuck hiding in an old oak stump next to the big shed, coaxing it out took ages but she was very happy to be taken back to the shed. Whilst getting her out I had heard more movement and returning found another two squeezed in the narrow gap between sheds, they were really difficult to get out as one end was blocked with a drainpipe and the other with brambles. Armed with a runner bean cane and very long arms Mick was able to jolly them along to me and another two chucks were safely returned to the hut.

Another chuck was found hiding behind the log shed. Mick managed to get the one in the holly bush with the aid of a broom whilst I went over old ground to find the last two. One I found pretending to be a log in the woodshed. Very well hidden under the pile, she was determined to stay put but in a dive worthy of a six nations penalty bid she was secured and hut bound. Mick and I joined forces for a final sweep. Nothing in the pig sty or log shed, under caravan or in the hedgerows. Just as we started to get despondent we heard faint clucking which led us to a big split oak stump against the old shed. Mick helped me ease into the gap to check, holding my legs whilst I squeezed further down between the block wall and tree trunk until I could finally see a tail end at the back of the hollow. This chuck was obviously part Ostrich, convinced no one could see her because her head was buried and she was determined to stay put. Now almost upside down and with the blood rushing to my head I finally grabbed a leg and pulled her out. Now Mick had to pull us both out as I was now firmly stuck! After what seemed like an age, I was pulled out and happy to be upright. A final check of the chicken hut now revealed a full roost, no deaths, and no injuries just nine shell-shocked chucks. We owed a big vote of thanks to the cavalry crows for coming to their rescue, twice now they had defended the chucks and I for one was happy to have them as neighbours.

Soaking in a well deserved and much needed hot bath the scratches and cuts from holly bush and brambles together with aching backs gradually eased. Warmed up and sat in front of a blazing fire, armed with respective glasses of wine and cider, we wound down and looking back on the day agreed we wouldn't have it any other way. No day the same, every one a revelation and guaranteed not to be repeated. Simple truism, each day you get a new present, whatever it is or however it makes you feel needn't faze you as the next day you get a new present to enjoy all over again. A definite case for living one day at a time, cue for a song, "One day at a time Sweet Jesus"! Quickly muffled by Mick throwing a cushion at me, my voice definitely no longer (if ever) able to carry a tune.

Later, lying in bed watching the stars and listening to the owls doing their rounds we carried on with our reflections. We realised it was now three years since our arrival in the valley and in that time we had changed from reliant townies into self sufficient country folk and we felt truly happy and content with our lot. Downsizing and going back to basics was definitely working for us. Less is definitely more as far as reducing stress is concerned. Identifying what was important to us and concentrating on things which were within our control to change had been the hardest challenge, now we were at last truly living life rather than just planning how to. We had finally found our way and were happy to live it to the full, one day at a time.